HUNTER
&Onyx

An Unconditional Love Story

A NOVEL BY

B. LOVE

© 2017

Published by Royalty Publishing House

www.royaltypublishinghouse.com

ALL RIGHTS RESERVED

PROLOGUE

*P*astor Stanford had never been a man who explained himself. Nor did he involve people in his plans or desires. Not because he was selfish or prideful or out for self… but because he learned early on in his ministerial career that everyone at your side does not have your back.

Some of those who have your back wish to be in your shoes. Some who say they're praying for you are actually praying against you. Not because of their hatred of you… but because of their love for self. Sure, they may want you to succeed… but not more than them.

When Pastor Stanford learned that hard and painful lesson, he began to make his moves in silence. After praying to God, and the peace that overwhelmed him as confirmation, he would turn his faith into works – speaking of them only after they came into fruition as a testimony.

But this current task was one that he had to let two people in on. Two people who had the weight to destroy all that he was prepared to build.

Pastor Stanford sat at his desk, massaging his temples as he waited for Carlton and Shantel Hendrix to arrive. Carlton had been a loyal and devote member of his church since he was a child. Shantel, since they were married well over thirty years ago. He could tell they were sincere in their walk with Christ, and that was the only reason he didn't stubbornly try to see his plan through without their involvement.

Light taps against his door caused him to lift his head and stare at it for a few seconds before ordering them to come in. Pastor Stanford stood and greeted them. All sitting at the same time.

"I thank you both for taking the time to come and see me. This won't take long," he started while pulling a picture closer to him. "You two know my granddaughter, Onyx, don't you?"

He looked from the picture to Carlton and Shantel.

"I remember the young version of Onyx. I haven't seen or heard anything about her in years. Is she okay?" Carlton inquired.

Pastor Stanford smiled with his eyes only as he put the picture back on his desk – away from their eyes. No one could see his granddaughter but him. He had always been protective of her. His absence from her life over the years may have caused her to think otherwise, but Pastor Stanford had always held a special place in his heart for his one and only grandchild.

"Depends on what you would call okay. It's time for me to find a successor. Well, I already have a successor. As you both know, the tradition here at The Dwelling Place is that all Pastors and Bishops remain of the Stanford bloodline. Either by birth or by marriage... preferably birth and blood."

Carlton sat deeper in his seat. As if he knew where Pastor Stanford was going with this.

"Your youngest son, Hunter, he's single correct?"

Carlton and Shantel looked at each other before Carlton spoke.

"He is."

"I'm coming to you because I know that he's a respectable young man and he values your input in his life. I don't want you two to stand in the way of what God is trying to do in his life."

"And what is God trying to do exactly, Pastor Stanford?" Shantel asked, ignoring the stare of her husband.

"Onyx... Onyx is my only grandchild. She's to be the First Lady of this church. In order for that to happen she needs a husband."

"She needs to get saved and have a relationship with God," Shantel countered quickly as she sat up in her seat.

"Shantel..." Carlton called softly.

"No. Pastor, I know that your granddaughter is one subject that you've forbad the members of this church to discuss... but this very church is on the line if you're considering putting her at the forefront. She's..."

"She's what?" Pastor Stanford asked with a louder tone as he leaned forward into his desk. "She's what, Sister Hendrix?"

Shantel sat back in her seat and looked at Carlton to speak for her.

"Pastor Stanford, it's no secret that your granddaughter is still in the world. That she used to sleep with men for money like a prostitute. That she strips for a living. Do you want a prostitute turned stripper turned First Lady to head your congregation?"

Pastor Stanford smiled and stood.

"It's not about what I want. It's about what God wants. Like I said... she needs a husband. Hunter. I don't need the two of you... especially you..." Pastor Stanford pointed at Shantel. "Standing in the way of what God is going to build with their union. Yes, I know she's in the world. Yes, I know she isn't saved. Yes, I know she might not be your top pick for your son, but need I remind you who he was before he came to church?

A gang banging dope pushing and using young thug in and out of jail. So, this will be the last time you ever speak of my granddaughter's profession as if that's what defines her. She is a child of God just as you are... she just... needs to come back home. And your son is how God is going to do that."

He sat as Carlton spoke.

"Listen, I hear you... and if God wants them together there is nothing we can do to stop it... but you have to understand our reservations about this. We've prayed and fasted for years to pull Hunter out of this worldly lifestyle, and you want us to just okay him being with a woman who can pull him back in?"

"Oh ye of little faith. Why is your first thought of him failing? Do you not believe in God or your son?"

"Why, though? If Onyx is the one you want in that position, why not seek to have her saved so she can run the church herself?" Shantel questioned.

"Have I ever steered you wrong before?" She shook her head no and lowered her eyes. "I'm not going to start now. It will take a certain kind of man to pull my granddaughter back to where she belongs. A man of God with a street edge. A man who can control and handle her. Not back down. Get her to submit. There aren't too many of those in this church. She needs a man who will be a man. This is an honor whether, your doubtful eyes can see it or not."

"We're grateful that you've chosen our son to lead your flock on your behalf," Carlton offered.

"I just don't understand why he needs him," Shantel mumbled as she disconnected herself from the conversation and situation. "Because he's a man?"

"Yes. Because he's a man. Men are designed to lead. But women are designed to influence their men's mind and vision. God will use Hunter to lead… but He will get to Hunter through Onyx." Pastor Stanford's eyes returned to the picture of her on his desk.

"When they told me they were naming her Onyx I asked them why. Onyx is a gemstone. A strong black stone. And they said they named her that because that's what she was going to be. A precious stone. A delicate yet strong woman. One who will shine even brighter when she's cut and polished. She's been cut. This life that she's led has shaped her. Now it's time for her to be polished. Cultivated into who she was born to be. Hunter is going to do that."

"You have our approval and our word that we won't stand in the way," Carlton said standing.

"Wait. What?" Shantel protested as she stood.

Carlton ignored her and held his hand out for Pastor Stanford to shake.

"Just one more question."

"What's that, Carlton?"

"You're only seventy and you're in perfect health and sound mind. Why are you ending your time as Pastor?"

Pastor Stanford smiled.

"It's not about me ending my time, son. It's about the beginning of theirs."

Hunter

This past week sleep had robbed me. I'd woken up at the same times every night. Midnight. Three AM. Five AM. My alarm doesn't sound until seven. By the time it does I'm just at that point of deep sleep that I need to feel refreshed throughout my day. So, instead of being refreshed I've gone through this past week restless.

I tried going to sleep later and that didn't help. I tried going to sleep earlier and that didn't help either. I stopped eating before bed and that just made me hungry and dehydrated by the time I woke up.

Nearing my breaking point, I called my Pastor for advice. He told me that I was being awakened to be awakened. That the longer I ignored the subtle pushing from God to get up I'd continue to suffer from restless nights. As Eli told Samuel in the bible, Pastor Stanford told me when I woke up to let the Lord know I was here and awake. Ready for whatever it was He was trying to get my attention to say.

I did, but he ain't say a thang back to me! I prayed and got out of bed. Opened my bible and sat at my desk for about an hour. Waiting for Him to put something on my heart, but it remained empty. It was too loud. In the dead of night, it was too loud. I threw on some basketball shorts and a wrinkled t-shirt and headed to the church to see if that would quiet the noise within me.

I never thought I'd be this type of man.

Running to the church in the middle of the night for clarity.

See, when I was a young nigga, I used to get into all kinds of trouble. I was an active gang member, and I was completely devoted to my set. We smoked and sold weed together. We robbed and fought together. I got into so much trouble that it got to the point where I wasn't even allowed in some places because they knew if I was around it was bound to be trouble.

I think my attitude came from being a light skinned young nigga. My parents had been in the church and stressed having a personal relationship with God all my life. And in my younger days it was cool… but by the time I hit thirteen I started seeing things differently.

I was getting picked on because I was a light skinned pretty youngin' with good hair and pink lips. They thought I was soft. They thought I couldn't handle myself. So I had to get my weight up and show them that that wasn't the case. My older brothers had a rep for themselves, but we were so far apart in age that we didn't go to the same middle and high school together. I was pretty much on my own. Until I joined my gang. They gave me the nickname Ali cause I was light skinned and I fought good; just like Muhammad Ali.

But anyway, I got into some things I shouldn't have. In the wrong place at the wrong time. At fifteen, I was hit with a manslaughter charge. Did seven years. Got out… and the first place I went was church. I told the Lord if He kept me out of trouble from that point forward I'd get my life together. It wasn't easy, but I did. Pastor Stanford had an Attorney friend to pull some strings for me and help me get enrolled at Tennessee State University. I got my Bachelors in Broadcasting two years ago. I've been the head of our media department at church and on the production team at Fox 13 ever since.

I guess you could say my life is what they would call a success. To go from the streets to a man of God with a legal well-paying job and a nice side hustle of directing videos and short films on the side is a life most aren't able to claim and see.

When I made it to the church I saw a car outside, but it didn't really faze me. I figured somebody was having car trouble earlier and just left it there or something. When I walked inside of the sanctuary and saw a woman on the altar I stopped immediately.

She stood and looked at the side exits. As if she was thinking about leaving before allowing me the opportunity to see her face. I started walking towards her. Not too many had keys to the church. And from behind she looked like no one who did. By the time I'd made it a few feet away from her she turned around to face me.

I stopped walking immediately.

Her face... was unfamiliar yet familiar at the same time. Her frame was slim yet toned. She had small yet ample breasts, and a flat stomach... standing in front of me like she wasn't the most beautiful woman I'd ever seen.

With tattoos covering her right arm and hand, weed red and tight eyes, a septum piercing, and deep green hair that was cut into a bob... there was a roughness about her that I found myself attracted to.

Yet her peanut butter colored skin, full heart shaped lips that parted at the sight of me, and long curly eyelashes made her look feminine.

She was confusing.

I watched as she licked her lips and I inadvertently licked mine.

"What are you doing here? How'd you get in?" I asked taking a step closer.

She took a step back and wrapped her arms around herself. I thought it may have been because she was scared, but I inhaled the scent of her marijuana perfume and figured it was probably because she was ashamed.

"How you gonna come up in here questioning me?" Was her slick response in a voice that reminded me of the calmness of Janet Jackson, yet the softness of a teenage girl.

"I just know that no one has a key but a select handful of the members of this church. I've never seen you before. So who are you?"

Her hand rose to her head as she scratched her scalp and inhaled deeply.

"Ask about me," she mumbled as she tried to walk past me.

I wrapped my hand around her wrist and pulled her back in front of me. For a few seconds we just looked at each other. I *really* looked at her. That's when it hit me.

Onyx

The forbidden topic of The Dwelling Place church. Pastor Stanford's granddaughter. She was nothing like I thought she'd be.

"Does he know you're here?" I asked letting go of her wrist.

She looked down at it like I'd branded her. Like she missed the feel of my skin against hers already.

"No, and you're not going to tell him either."

"Why not? He'd be happy to know…"

"I don't want him to know. I come here to pray before my shift and to feel a little closer to him and my grandma. I don't want him showing up ruining what I got going on."

"He misses you, Onyx."

The sound of her name on my lips caused her to look at my mouth and lick her full ones again. I put some space between us. I refused to lust after this woman in church.

"He doesn't have to miss me. He didn't have to disown me. That's what you Christians do. Preach love, yet judge and condemn people in hypocrisy. Like y'all don't sin. Or, you outcast those who aren't afraid to not hide theirs."

She tried to walk away again. I grabbed her forearm. This time a little tighter. This time I pulled her a little closer. This time she looked at me like I'd offended her. Frankly, I had no cares to give.

"First of all, don't put me in the same boat as them. You don't know me just like I don't know you. Second of all, watch the way you talk to me. I'll talk to you in love and you're going to talk to me with respect. Am I making myself clear?"

Onyx licked those lips again and bit down on the bottom one. I closed and opened my eyes quickly – praying she didn't feel the bulge growing between us. Between my thighs.

"Am I making myself clear?" I repeated.

I was ready to get this over with so I could put some space between us. She smirked and looked me up and down as best as she could before tilting her head to the side.

"Who are you?"

"Hunter. Hunter Hendrix."

Her smirk turned into a half smile as she nodded and tried to remove herself from me but I pulled her even closer.

"You better let me go, Hunter Hendrix. Before I have you smelling like weed."

"I'll take my chances."

"Why? You like being close to me?"

"I like being respected."

Her half smile turned into a full one.

"Why are you here?"

"Will you answer my original question so I can let you go?"

"You don't want to."

"What makes you think that?"

"Did you forget you're only wearing basketball shorts? I feel you."

I released her and took a step back.

"Listen, you seem like a cool guy, so I'll let you get away with putting your hands on me. Maybe you aren't like them. I ain't taking no chances, though. I'm cool with God. It's just His supposed children I can't deal with." She tried to walk away again and this time I let her. "And from here on out, do whatever you came here to do tonight somewhere else. At this time of night this church belongs to me and I don't share."

I turned around and watched her walk out of the church. I don't know how long I stood there smiling, but when I walked outside the sun was up. And my mind was clear.

*E*ver since I left him, Hunter Hendrix had been on my mind.

I remembered everything about him. His tall stature. His tan, golden skin. His low tapered cut and neatly trimmed beard. His close set coffee brown eyes. His piercing eyes. His pinkish brown lips. Those lips. I loved watching him lick those lips. He had the straightest teeth I'd ever seen.

But what I remember most – the feel of his skin against mine. The feel of his dick at my stomach. The way he handled me and commanded respect naturally.

I'd misjudged him. I didn't expect him to handle me the way he did. That was the first time anyone had ever come to the church during my nightly visits. It didn't surprise me that he knew who I was. I could only imagine what he'd heard about me. For the first time, I had the strongest urge to explain myself to him.

To tell him that half of what he heard was probably true… but all with good reason. There was something about him that I felt connected to. Something that told me that I could be me with him and he wouldn't judge me.

I hadn't let a man inside of my body or heart in three years, though – and I didn't plan on starting now.

Even though I was off from the club tonight I still decided to follow my usual routine. I stopped by Waffle House to eat and smoke a blunt before heading to the church to chat it up with God and look at the pictures of my parents and grandparents lining the church walls.

Off the clock I didn't wear my wig. My natural hair was out and in six French braids that stopped at the middle of my back. My face was bare of any makeup. I didn't even have my nose ring in. I dressed comfortably in sweats and a tank top with the multicolor Adidas slides one of my only two friends Riley got me for my birthday. Her brother Raj was my neighbor. If I wasn't hanging with one of them I stayed to myself.

I made it to church and was a little disappointed when I didn't see Hunter's car outside. I told him to stay away… but I was kind of hoping he didn't listen. No, I needed him to listen.

Fuck these feelings.

My eyes rolled at the sight of him sitting on the back pew. Irritation immediately filled me. Damn him for giving me what I wanted but didn't need.

"Thought I told you to go somewhere else?" I mumbled walking towards him.

He didn't answer me right away. Just stood and ran his fingers down one of my braids with a soft smile before pulling the end gently.

"I like you better like this," he spoke lowly.

I flicked his hand away and crossed my arms over my chest.

"I thought I told you to go somewhere else? Where is your car?"

"I parked in the back. I figured you wouldn't come in if you knew I was here."

"Why are you here?"

Hunter shrugged and sat back down. I leaned against the pew and looked down at him.

"You're not going to sit down?"

I shook my head no and twisted my top lip up. He sighed quietly and grabbed my hand to sit me down.

"You got a bad habit of putting your hands where they don't belong."

"Why you giving me such a hard time?"

"I don't know how to be no other way."

"That's a lie."

"How you figure that?"

"I can see it in your eyes, Onyx."

There he goes. Saying my name like that again. I lowered my eyes and head absently. Using the tips of his fingers, he lifted my head by my chin.

"I wanna watch you unfold," he continued in that same soft voice. Much gentler and inviting than the one he used last night. Or would that be considered this morning? Hell, I don't know.

"Ion have nothing to show."

"Another lie."

I pushed his hand from my face finally.

"There's a glow under you. Tucked deep inside. I get why you don't want to show anyone else… but you can show me. Those parts of you that no one else can see."

"Listen…"

"I'll be gentle with you, Onyx."

"Stop fu-"

This nigga had me damn near cursing in this church. I guess it didn't matter since I was thinking it anyway. God knows our hearts. Might as well be real and let it slip out. For some reason, I didn't want to offend Hunter Hendrix, though.

"Do I unnerve you?" he asked sitting sideways to face me.

"Yea. So stop."

He chuckled quietly and nodded.

"Tell me about you, Onyx."

"What do you want to know, Hunter Hendrix?"

"Why do you always say my full name?"

"Because I love the way it sounds."

"I love the way it sounds falling from your lips."

The silly smile that tried to spread across my face shocked me.

Was I blushing?

"What do you want to know?"

The look he gave me told me without him having to say a word. He didn't care about the basics of me. He just wanted to know was it true. And if it was, why. And after why, how could I be here right now. Maybe hearing about my current line of work and what led to it would put out whatever it was he thought he felt for me. Whatever had him growing hard at the feel of me.

"I guess I just want to know if it's all true."

I shrugged and lowered my gaze. Wishing I'd finished my blunt before I came in.

"I can't tell you if it's true if I don't know what you're talking about. Just say it."

He looked down in shame. Like he couldn't fix his mouth to say it. So to hurry this along I prepared to spill my guts to a nigga for the first time.

"I curse a lot. Can we take this conversation outside?" His eyes returned to mine. "I mean… unless that will offend you. In which case we probably should just end this conversation now."

Hunter stood and extended his hand for me. I placed my hand inside and allowed him to help me stand. We walked outside in silence. I walked over to my car and retrieved my half smoked blunt.

"Really, Onyx? On church grounds?"

"Do you want me to talk about this shit or not?"

"Yea, but you gotta do all that?"

Shrugging again, I put my arms to my sides and looked towards the sky.

"Fine," he mumbled, sticking his hand inside of my pocket and grabbing my keys.

I was about to curse his sexy ass out, but I liked him being close to me so I let it go. He walked over to the passenger side of my car and opened the door. I looked at him skeptically.

"Come on," he ordered snapping his fingers.

"Nigga, don't be snapping at me!"

"Just, come on, Onyx."

"Where?"

"Up the street. Ion want you doing all that on church grounds."

My skepticism faded and was replaced with surprise. Surprise because he didn't judge me or try to make me stop. He accepted me, yet refused to allow me to disrespect the house of God.

"Where we going?"

"Up the street to Waffle House."

"I ain't hungry."

"I am. So come on."

Why was I allowing this man to handle me this way? Unsure of why, I walked to the passenger side of my car and stared at him for a few seconds before he gently nudged my body inside. Hunter got inside of the driver's seat and pushed it back to his liking. The second he cut my car on Chance the Rapper started blasting through my speakers. I smiled as I waited to see his reaction. He didn't cut it off. He didn't change it to a gospel station. He simply looked over at me while cutting it down to a reasonable level.

"I ain't tryna change you, Onyx. So all those walls you got up you can let down."

What was I supposed to say to that shit? I just nodded and looked out of my window in silence.

Hunter

She said she wasn't hungry, but by the time we made it to Waffle House and she'd finished the rest of her blunt, she was ordering some food right along with me. We both got the patty melt. I got the meal but she only got the sandwich. Said she wanted just a little something to hold her over. While we waited for the food I gave her time to gather her thoughts.

Honestly, I didn't expect her to open up to me. Not this soon anyway. That led me to believe one of two things – either she didn't plan on talking to me ever again, or she wasn't as hard as she put out to be.

"So…" I mumbled, running my pointing finger under her chin.

Onyx smiled but let it fall quickly as she pushed my hand away. I had the hardest time keeping my hands off of her.

"So what, Hunter Hendrix?"

I swear the way she said my name made me feel like a man filled with power. A man with the greatest treasure sitting right before me. I'd heard that a person's name to that person was the most important word in any language… but hearing her say my name… made me feel like I'd never heard it be said before she spoke it.

"Talk to me."

"Let's just get this clear right now. My life is mine to live and I refuse to let anyone make me feel bad about it."

"I told you I ain't here to change you."

"Then why are you here, Hunter Hendrix?"

I pulled her move and shrugged before taking a sip of my water.

"Just… seems like this is where I need to be."

Onyx scratched the back of her neck and looked at me briefly before sitting back in her seat.

"I guess I had a normal church kid childhood. My parents and grandparents were in church practically every day. If they weren't at DP they were visiting someone else's church. Between that and school I was hardly ever at home except for Saturdays and those were set aside for resting.

I didn't have any siblings. No social life. I just… didn't feel… that loving bond that I thought I should have. I didn't feel loved and wanted. Accepted. So I rebelled. Started getting into trouble at school because that got me some attention when I got home. That didn't last long, though. They just… started ignoring me."

She smiled as her eyes glossed with tears.

"My grandpops told them to ignore me. That anything that they didn't feed would starve. That I would stop acting out if they didn't entertain my foolishness."

"Did you?"

"I did."

"So what happened?"

"I had a growth spurt and little niggas started seeing me and I gave up my virginity. Started getting what I thought was love and acceptance from them. Sex made me feel... close to another human being. I was just... so tired of feeling alone.

Yea, they say... God loves you. You're never alone. But I needed something I could *feel.* Arms to wrap around me. A voice that I could hear tell me that they love me."

She brushed her tear away. Like that would keep me from seeing it. Resisting the urge to walk over to her side of the table and hold her, I put my hands in my pockets. That's probably what she needed... but she seemed so guarded. I didn't think she would actually even allow me to.

"When I was eighteen, I was approached by this old ass dude. He was like forty something. I was driving and he pulled up on the side of me in this pretty ass corvette. I'm sitting there in my little Hyundai getting ready for college feeling like I'm the shit, right... but seeing that car made me feel like shit."

Onyx smiled nostalgically and shook her head.

"He was straight to the point with it. Told me he wanted to spoil me. Give me his time and money just to have me on his arm. Just to have my companionship. And the first thing on my mind is like... really, dude? You wanna pay me to give me something I've wanted my whole fucking life? I said yes of course.

He took me to the mall that day and blew three stacks on me. By the time I drained him I was on to the next. I couldn't stick around with one for too long. Made me feel... I don't know. Comfortable I guess. It was what I wanted, but I didn't want to get attached.

I didn't want it to hurt when they switched up on me and stopped giving me their all. So, by the time I was on my fifth sugar daddy, I was talking to one that was all into PDA. We were kissing and shit in the mall one day.

I went to the bathroom, and when I came out there was a younger nigga standing across from the door. He was like, 'You wanna use your body to make some real money without having to have sex with that old ass troll?' I said yea and that was that. It was Slimy. The owner of the strip club I work at.

He put me on as a dancer and I've been doing that ever since."

I must have stared at her for too long because she looked away and asked, "Did I scare you away?"

Instead of answering her, I stood and walked over to her side of the booth. She scooted over so I could sit down.

"No," I mumbled, running my fingers down her cheek before turning her to face me.

She looked at me like she didn't believe me. Like she expected me to judge her and tell her I didn't want to have anything else to do with her. Truth of the matter was; I didn't know what I wanted to do with her. All I knew was that she made my mind clear... and I needed that. I needed her. Her hand covered mine and she tried to pull it down but I kept it there.

"Why not?"

"Did you want it to?" Closing her eyes, she nodded yes. "Why?"

Onyx opened them but avoided mine.

"What do you want from me?"

"I don't want anything from you, Onyx. I need you."

Her eyes returned to mine.

"What kind of game you running?"

"None at all."

"Then what do you mean you need me?"

"Just what I said."

"You don't need me. You don't even know me."

"I know I haven't been able to sleep, but since I met you my mind has been clear and at ease. I know I slept better this morning than I had all week. I know being here with you right now has me so at peace I could lay my head on this table and be knocked out in thirty seconds. Honestly, I don't want you. You're no good for me. Your mouth is reckless. You got bad habits. And you're mean. But I need you."

"I'm mean? Well… you're stupid."

She pushed my hand away and tried to push me out of the booth but I sat firm.

"You're petty too, Onyx. You know I'm telling the truth. Don't get in your feelings."

"Get up so I can get out. And you're walking back to the church too."

"Girl, please."

"Hunter, let me out."

"What happened to Hunter Hendrix?"

Her eyes squinted. Her eyebrows lowered. My smile widened.

"Move, nigga."

"What if I don't?"

"I'm gonna climb over this table and leave."

"Ion believe you."

The words hadn't even fallen out of my mouth before her crazy self was putting her feet on the seat and trying to climb on top of the table. I grabbed her and tossed her over my shoulder.

"Hunter! Put me down!"

I ignored her as I pulled my wallet out of my pocket. After tossing a twenty on the table to cover the food we hadn't even gotten yet I carried her outside.

"I ain't got on my shoes!" she yelled as I walked outside.

"Ion care. You should've thought about that before you started acting a fool."

"Boy, you better go get my damn shoes! Those are my favorite shoes!"

I unlocked her car and put her in the driver's seat.

"Go get my shoes, Hunter."

After slamming her door, I went back into the restaurant to get her shoes. I opened the passenger door and tossed them onto the seat. Then I started my walk back to the church. It took her a few seconds to start her car and pull up behind me. I guess she couldn't believe what

I'd just done. When she saw that I wasn't going to stop walking she pulled up on the side of me and rolled her window down.

"I can take you back to the church. It's dark out here," she offered softly.

"Nah, I'm good."

"So your stubborn ass gon walk outside in the dark just because you don't want to get in the car with me?"

I stopped walking. She stopped driving.

"Ain't that what you told me to do?"

Her eyes rolled in the darkness and she massaged her right temple. Like I was the one being difficult. Like I was giving her a headache.

"I can take you back to the church."

"Nah, I'm good."

My slow pace continued. Her driving continued.

"Fine!" she yelled before speeding off.

"Fine!" I yelled after her.

I don't know who she thought she was dealing with... but she would learn soon enough... I might be a man of God, but I'm still a man. And she will respect me.

Onyx

I found myself waiting for him. Waiting for him to come to this church and get under my skin. But I had only five minutes left before I needed to leave for the club and he hadn't arrived yet.

Maybe I'd finally run him off.

But he... he scared me.

Looking into my eyes like that. Talking to me like that. Touching me like that. So sincere. So genuine. He read me. I wasn't used to that obviously. And he... he didn't sugarcoat shit with me. He called me out like he ain't give a fuck. This church going pretty boy called me out like it was nothing.

Yea, I can be petty. I can be a little mean. I do some things I probably shouldn't. But no man has ever cared enough or had the balls to call me out on it.

Except for Hunter Hendrix.

And that scared me.

Looking at my phone for the last and final time, I slid it in my pocket and let out a disappointed breath as I stood from the altar and began my walk down the aisle. The doors creaked opened and I stopped walking immediately. My heart stopped beating momentarily.

He came!

Yo, chill out.

My hands went down my face as I inhaled deeply.

I should probably apologize.

I'm not, though.

I saw him… and I wanted to run into his arms. To punch his fine ass for making me wait so long. I couldn't move. My feet were planted. He shook his head at me as he walked towards me. I'm sure he thought I was being difficult, but I literally couldn't move at the sight of him.

As soon as he made his way to me his fingers wrapped around mine. Using his free hand, he caressed my cheek. Causing me to close my eyes and try to push my chills back in if it be at all possible.

I heard, "What took you so long?" come from me. From my voice. I opened my eyes. Furrowed my brows in confusion. *Did I just ask him that?* I guess I did because he smiled as he pulled me closer.

"I started not to come," Hunter admitted.

"Why not?"

He shrugged as his fingers glided over my lips. God, I wanted him to kiss me.

"I need to go, Onyx."

"Why?"

No, why was my voice this ragged? This desperate. *Why did I feel so needy?*

"It's… I need to go."

"No, you don't need to go. You want to go. You said you needed me. How can you need me and need to be away from me at the same time?"

"I need to be away from you because I need you. This is too much. Way too soon. And you won't let me in."

But I will.

"I don't know how."

"Will you let me teach you?"

Taking a step back, I rubbed my sweaty palms together. I needed to get to the club. If I was late again, Slimy would make me go on as soon as I arrived. I loved making them wait. The added anticipation had them twice as excited to see me and willing to peel off those bills.

"I have to go. I need to get to work."

"You can't even say it, so how are you going to do it?"

"I can't have a heart to heart with you right now, Hunter Hendrix. You're the one who took so long getting here. I have to go."

He didn't say something smart like I thought he would. He just smiled and nodded.

"I guess I'll see you tomorrow, Onyx."

I nodded and licked my lips. He stood there and looked at me for a few seconds before leaving. I sat at the nearest pew and took a few breaths to compose myself. To give the smile I'd been holding in time to come out. *He came.* When I felt like myself I stood and started my walk out.

The doors opened again and I thought maybe he'd changed his mind… but it was the gas station attendant from across the street. My smile fell as I walked towards him.

"You need to leave so I can lock up," I ordered softly.

"I thought the doors of the church were always open?" he asked with a crooked smile.

"Not this late they aren't. Come back in the morning."

"Actually, I came for you. I see you in here every night. I was just... wondering... if... I could... get..."

Refusing to believe he was about to ask me for a dance in this church, I shook my head and motioned for him to get out with my hand.

"Get out before you make me lose what little morality I have."

"But I have money." He pulled a wad of wrinkled bills from his pocket. "I just got paid today."

My smile returned as I chuckled in disbelief.

"It's time for you to go."

"So you're not going to give me a dance?"

"No."

I watched as he scratched the side of his mouth and stared at me.

"Why not?"

"We're in a church. Come down to the club and I'll see what I can do."

Lord, forgive me for lying in church.

"I don't believe you. I came last week and asked for a private dance, but they told me I didn't have enough to even retain you. You're that uppity that you have a flat fee before you even dance for a man? So what that mean? I don't have to tip you?"

He stuffed his money back in his pants and took a step towards me. I took a step back. I feared no nigga, but I wasn't a fool. He was twice my size and obviously not there all the way in the head to think he was going to get a lap dance in a church.

I might have been a little twisted, but I'd never be that sick.

"No, you'd still have to tip me. Get at me when you get your money up."

I tried to walk past him but he gripped my forearm. Hard. His touch was different. No... his touch was the same as every other man that had touched me. But... it showed me that Hunter's touch was different. That he touched me in a way that no man ever had. Even when Hunter pulled me close to him firmly, there was still a gentleness and care within his touch that I felt with no one else.

"Ima need you to let me go."

"Not until I get my dance."

Jerking away from him did nothing but cause him to hold me tighter. Losing my cool, I inhaled deeply and closed my eyes.

"I'm not asking you again."

"Neither am I. I want my dance."

He turned me around and wrapped his arms around my waist from behind.

"Nigga, if you don't get your ass off of me!" I yelled elbowing him.

Quickly he covered his eye in disbelief as I speedily walked away from him. By the time I made my way to the door he was grabbing my neck and yanking me down to the ground. The shit surprised me and discombobulated me a little.

He jumped on top of me, but I kicked him in the groin and pulled the knife I always carried in the back pocket of my sweats. Before he could compose himself, I slid my knife over his cheek. He yelped in pain as I kicked where I'd cut.

I spit on him and straightened my shirt before walking out of the church. I started to lock him inside, but I kept the doors open so he could crawl his sorry ass out.

Fuck what he thought this was. Nobody got a dance or the pussy for free.

Hunter

I found myself waiting for her. She never came. By the time it hit three in the morning I decided to call it a night. Maybe something came up. Maybe I scared her away. Maybe she was tired of playing with me. Maybe she overslept. Maybe something was wrong.

Standing, I shook the thoughts from my head and walked down the aisle of the church. When I made it a few feet away from the door I noticed blood. That wasn't there when I left yesterday. That didn't sit well with me.

Was she sick? Had someone come in after I left? I pulled my phone from my pocket and searched for Slimy in Memphis. A picture came up of a dark skinned guy who looked to be in his thirties. He was on a nightlife blog listed as the owner of Uncle Slimy's Palace. Clicking the link for the directions, I made my way to the club.

I wouldn't be able to sleep until I saw her and knew that she was okay.

The club was about thirty minutes away from the church. When I pulled up and saw her car I felt a little more at ease, but I still needed to see *her*. Onyx was behind the bar all smiles talking to the bartender. I started walking towards her.

She must have saw me out the corner of her eye because she

looked at me and her smile was replaced with sadness as she pointed towards an empty table behind me. I sat down and watched as she whispered something in the DJ's ear. The song changed to Erykah Badu's *I Want You.*

Her smile returned as she sauntered over to me. As Erykah sung about wanting a man. Asking what they were going to do. How she wanted him in the worst kind of way.

Finally, she made her way to the VIP section I was in. I didn't want to stare at her body so hard, but what else could I do with it right there in front of me? I appreciated the fact that she had on a crop top and high waist shorts, but I knew that wasn't what she was going to be dancing in.

With one six-inch pump on the step, Onyx stared at me. Like she was giving me time to let the words of the song seep into my head. The words about love being on the way and it not letting go. How I could pray 'til early May and fast for thirty days and it still wouldn't let go. She smirked as she finally walked in front of me. The chair was already pushed back and turned to the side.

I closed my eyes as Erykah repeated that she wanted him. As she repeatedly asked what they were going to do. Her body sat across mine and I gripped her waist absently.

Onyx pulled feelings and desires out of me that no other woman ever had. Even in my younger days.

Her arms stretched around me as she gripped the back of my chair. Her waist circled on top of me. My head flew back as I gripped her tighter.

This was wrong. This wasn't what I came here for. I came for her, but not like this. Not like this. Her legs flew up. Her ankles wrapped around my neck. Her back went to my thighs. Her... her... the essence of what made her a woman lifted, and she twirled it around in my face just as she'd done on my waist.

My hands went to the sides of her shorts and I tugged at them. I tugged at them. Like I wanted to take them off. If I had this kind of reaction to her I could only imagine what the rest of these niggas felt like watching her.

Quickly, I removed her ankles from my neck and put her legs around my waist as I stood and carried her out of the VIP section.

"Where you taking me?" Onyx asked with a small smile.

With her being this close I could really look in her eyes. She'd had a couple of drinks. Her eyes were resting low. Not drunk low... but low like she'd reached her limit of what she could drink before feeling any real effects.

"Home. You're done here."

"What? Hunter I..."

"Just, be quiet, Onyx."

Her hands ran down the back of my neck, and I tossed half of her body over my shoulder to keep her from touching me.

"You gon get enough of handling me like this," I heard her warn from behind me.

"Whatever."

"O... you good?" The bouncer at the door asked.

"Yea. I'm good. Can you call to the back and tell Shy to bring my shit outside? He said I'm done for the night."

"Nah, you done for good," I corrected carrying her outside.

"Mane… gone on with that shit."

I ain't even say anything to her. I let her think whatever she wanted to at this point as I put her in my car. I looked at her briefly until I saw a curvy chick come outside and look around.

"Is that Shy?" I asked.

Onyx looked at the door and back to me without saying anything. Taking that as a yes, I closed the passenger door and went to retrieve her belongings. Ole girl told me to tell Onyx to call her when she got home and I nodded before making my way back to my car. I opened her biggest bag and pulled a pair of sweats and tank top from it.

When I opened the door I tossed them at her and put the rest of her stuff in the backseat.

"I need some shoes unless you want me walking around in sweats and pumps."

"I like the pumps."

"Give me my shoes, Hunter."

I groaned and grabbed her shoes and handed them to her. She gave me her address and I put it in my GPS. We didn't speak until I pulled up in front of her apartment.

"I'll take you to get your car in the morning once your drinks have worn off. What happened?" I asked cutting my car off.

"I'll get my neighbor to take me. What you talking about?"

"At church."

She looked out of the window and into the darkness.

"I handled it."

"You handled it?" I almost yelled. Sitting back in my seat, I prayed quickly and quietly to calm myself down. "What did you handle, Onyx?"

"This nigga came in trying to get me to dance for him."

"In the church? She nodded and turned slightly away from me in her seat. "Why was there blood on the carpet? Did he touch you?"

"We tussled a little. The blood is from me cutting him."

"He didn't…"

"No. He didn't rape me. Like I said… I took care of it."

I started my car back up.

"Do you know where he is?"

Her head turned quickly.

"Why?"

"Do you know where he is?"

"Well… yea… but I told you…"

"Where is he, Onyx?"

"This is a part of this industry sadly. Niggas think they're entitled to take what they want when they want it."

"I don't care. That's not right. And it ain't happening to you. Where is he?"

She sat back in her seat and massaged her temples.

"At the gas station across from the church."

I nodded and reversed. If I had to sit up there until he arrived… that's what I was going to do. But this was about to be handled immediately.

Onyx

*T*he sight of Hunter at the club made me feel some type of way. Ways actually. I was happy. Turned on. Sad. Embarrassed. Needy. Ugh. Too much. He was right – this was too much too soon. I hadn't told anyone about what happened and I didn't plan on telling anyone. Leave it up to him to see that nigga's blood and come hunting me down to find out what happened.

I wasn't expecting him to look for him. I thought he'd be like… you need to go file a police report. Or tell me that's what I get for stripping. Or tell me I needed to be more careful. But he pulled up to the gas station showing me a side of him I'd never seen before.

"Don't open that door," he ordered.

I pulled my hand from the handle and waited for him to come and open it for me. When he did, we walked into the gas station.

"Point him out to me."

"Hunter… you really don't have to…"

The look he gave me shut me up. I looked around and saw him putting cases of beer in the fridge.

"He's over there," I mumbled.

"Where?" I pointed towards the cooler. "Okay. Go back to the car."

"Hunter, I'm not going back…"

My words fell on deaf ears as he walked away from me and towards the creep. I expected him to talk to him. To threaten him. To try and make him apologize. Hunter nudged his shoulder to get his attention. I couldn't hear what they said but it of course was something about me because he pointed towards me.

The creep shook his head adamantly. He must have been trying to deny it. Hunter pointed at the cut on his face and he still was shaking his head no. To my total and complete surprise, Hunter swung on him and knocked him down with one punch.

I grabbed the display of chips on the side of me and tried to compose myself. My panties got wet. My knees grew weak. *Why was the sight of him protecting me turning me on so damn much?* It was like something turned off inside of him. He started kicking the defenseless creep who was unconscious and unable to defend himself.

"Hunter!" I yelled. He stopped immediately. "That's enough." His eyes met mine and he nodded – but continued to stand there. "Let's go."

Hunter took a step back and looked around before walking towards me. He grabbed me by my forearm and pulled me out of the store.

"Didn't I tell you to go back to the car?"

"I… you… I'm glad I didn't. You would've killed him. Why did you do that? Where did that even come from?"

He smiled as he opened the door for me.

"I ain't been saved all my life." Was his soft and simple reply.

I couldn't even get in the car. All I could do was stare at him. All I could do was want to know him. In every way possible.

"Get in," he said softly.

I nodded but still didn't move. Why was he always leaving me frozen? Hunter pushed me deeper into the car until my body was touching it. He lifted my left leg and put it in the car. I took care of the rest. The ride back to my place was silent as I stared at the side of his face. Every once in a while he'd look over at me and smile, causing me to look away.

By the time he pulled up to my apartment I didn't know what to say. What to feel. How to act.

"Thanks," I offered.

"No thanks needed. It's my job to protect you."

"How is it your job to protect me?"

"Are you going to let me take you out or not?"

"Not. I don't date church boys. Or fine men."

"What? So, you think I'm fine?"

I looked over at him and took in his features as he smiled.

"You know you're fine, Hunter Hendrix."

"So you saying you only date ugly men?"

"Yea. Cute niggas cheat. They flirt too much."

"That ain't me."

"And church boys are boring."

"Is there anything about me that seems boring to you, Onyx?"

I looked at him again and licked my lips. *Not at all.*

"All the same. I don't date church boys or fine men. And you're both. What do you want with me anyway? Haven't you read the scripture about being unequally yoked?"

"You could be a Christian and we could still be unequally yoked, Onyx. Don't play. You know that."

I shrugged and looked out of the window. Hunter got out and came to my side of the car. He opened the door and grabbed my bags as I got out.

"You really didn't have to do that, but thanks."

"I don't want you stripping no more. You need to quit. Today. That doesn't even count as something you can put on your resume so you don't have to put in two weeks' notice. I don't want you going back, Onyx."

"Why not, Hunter Hendrix?"

"Because I don't want no other nigga looking at what's mine. Touching what's mine. Lusting over what's mine. You got my Holy Spirit all of whack over this mess. That's not the environment you belong in."

"I just told you I'm not dating you."

"All the same you're done. You can date other men until you realize what you have in me. But you bet not kiss them. And don't even think about having sex with them."

"Nigga…"

"You belong to me." As if he was giving that time to resonate within me he paused. "I'll give you time to realize that. In the meantime, no more stripping. When we get married you won't have to work. Until then, you need to find another job. If I have to cover your bills until you find one-"

"I have money saved, Hunter."

He smiled and nodded his approval.

"Good." I watched as he pulled his phone from his pocket. "Take this off," he said pulling at my wig.

"For what?"

"I want a picture of you for your contact ID."

"I am *not* taking a picture with some braids going down my head."

"But I told you I like you better like that anyway."

"Why?"

"Because it's the real you."

His fingers tried to slide under my wig and I pushed them away.

"Stop before you snatch my edges."

"Take it off then."

"I am!"

I carefully pulled the clips from my hair and removed the wig. As soon as I did he smiled and grabbed it.

"There go my baby."

"Hunter, stop," I pleaded through my blush.

"Aight."

He took a step back and held his camera up.

I threw up my middle finger with a mug on my face and he shook his head with a smile as he took the picture.

"So this what you want me to show my family when they ask me who's stolen my heart and attention?"

Leaning back on his car, I licked my lips and bit the bottom one.

"What's your number?" he continued without giving me a chance to answer his original question. I didn't have an answer anyway.

I grabbed his phone and locked my number in.

"Promise me you won't go back, Onyx."

I handed him his phone and let out a hard breath. I wasn't sure if that was something I could promise him. Yea, I was kind of over the lifestyle, but at the same time I had a lifestyle to maintain. And I lived off the attention I received. The love. But out of all the men I'd ever called myself loving… none of them took care of me the way Hunter was beginning to.

None of them gave me the attention and care he did.

The protection he did.

The stimulation he did.

If I had to turn away from that artificial love and life to get real love and attention from this genuine man… so be it.

"I give you my word, Hunter Hendrix."

Hunter stepped towards me and my chest and stomach caved in as I pushed myself deeper into his car.

"Relax, you know I ain't gone take it there with you," he mumbled before kissing my forehead sweetly. "Bet not no other nigga take it there with you either. Don't play with me, Onyx. You see I don't play."

I smiled and decided to let him have the last word for a change. He walked me to my front door and sat my bags down.

"Call me when you get home. Or text me. Just text me," I rushed out.

"I will. Be safe, Onyx. I'll see you later."

"When?"

He smiled and took a step back.

"When would you like to?"

"You gotta ask me out on a date, don't you?"

"I just did. You shot me down."

"Oh yea. That's right. Well… I guess I'll see you at church."

He looked away briefly before returning his eyes to me.

"Sounds perfect. Perfect."

I waited until he left before going inside of my apartment, throwing my shit on the couch, and texting Riley 911. She would not believe all I had to tell her.

Hunter

All of my late nights are early mornings with Onyx were beginning to weigh me down. I was light and at peace, yea, but I was… restless. I needed a full night of sleep. So much so that I completely slept through my alarm last night. I texted Onyx and apologized for my absence, and in true nonchalant uncaring Onyx fashion she hit me with an unconcerned emoji.

I started to call her and reschedule for another night, but I decided to do that in person. Had I called or texted her she would've found a way to say no. But there wasn't too much she could say no to when she was in my face.

Not because she was weak or anything like that, but because my masculine energy was something that she needed so much in her life that she just… couldn't resist it. Couldn't resist me.

So, imagine my surprise when I made it to my job and she was there. Waiting for me. She had two cups of coffee and two pastry bags sitting next to her as she smoked a blunt. Onyx put the blunt out and stood at the sight of me. Her dimples were caving in as she tried to hide her smile.

"Hey," she spoke softly. "I probably look like a stalker or some shit, huh?"

I couldn't even answer her right away. I was so surprised... all I could do was look at her with what felt like the biggest smile on my face.

"I wanted to stop by and bring you something. Nothing big. Just... as another thank you for what you did."

She handed me one of the pastry bags as she continued.

"I didn't know what you like, so I got you a piece of banana bread. I have a birthday cake pop for breakfast like every other day so..."

Onyx shrugged and lowered her head.

"Will you say something?"

I took a step towards her, and when she tried to take a step back, I grabbed her by the back of her neck and pulled her into my chest. She looked up at me with those tightened eyes and closed them as she licked her lips.

"Hunter..."

"You tryna make me make you fall in love with me, huh?"

Onyx opened her eyes immediately and flashed that cocky smile I'd gotten used to.

"Boy, bye. I was just trying to be nice."

"You can't be doing this type of stuff, Onyx. This is the type of stuff that makes a man feel appreciated. And if you make a man feel appreciated... he caters to you. Is that what you want me to do?"

She shook her head adamantly as her eyebrows wrinkled and her eyes closed. My hand went from her neck to her cheek and I brushed it gently with my thumb. The urge to kiss her was hitting me so strongly, and I knew she had to feel the effect she had on me growing between my legs, but I couldn't pull myself to do it.

I knew that I had to take things extremely slow with Onyx. There were so many guards around her heart that I had to make my way through mentally, emotionally, and spiritually before I felt comfortable doing anything with her physically.

Not even a small kiss.

"Thank you, baby. You made my day with this act of kindness. I appreciate this a lot."

Her eyes opened and met mine and she smiled softly.

"No problem. I won't hold you. I just… wanted to drop that off."

I nodded, but kept my hand on her cheek.

"Your coffee's probably already cold."

I nodded, but kept my hand on her cheek.

"Hunter Hendrix, will you let me go?"

"You don't want me to."

"What makes you think that?"

"Your hand is wrapped around my wrist rather tightly for someone that wants me to let them go."

Onyx looked at her hand, like she hadn't even realized she was touching me, then she removed it quickly and took a step back. My thumb slid across her bottom lip without my permission and she inhaled a sharp breath that made me take a step back and put my hands in my pockets.

"Ima uh, go on in. We're going out tonight."

"Are you asking me out on a date? Hunter, I told you that I didn't want to…"

I took a step towards her and placed my pointing finger over her lips.

"I wasn't really asking you, Onyx. I'm telling you that I'm taking you out tonight. So be ready at seven."

"Fine," she mumbled as she slapped my hand away from her face.

Onyx grabbed her coffee and walked away from me, mumbling under her breath with an attitude the whole time. I stood there and watched with a crooked smile until she was in her car and on her way out.

Onyx

My day had quickly turned to shit when I saw the drained expression on Hunter's face as his parents walked behind him. His mother's lips were moving fast as hell while his father shook his head in annoyance, and I could only imagine what his mother was saying.

Hunter called me about an hour ago and told me that he'd been arrested.

Okay, so let me back track.

Who did he think he was telling me that he was going to take me out tonight? Like he just knew I was going to be okay with that. Shit, to be honest, Hunter Hendrix could've told me to follow him to the moon at this point and I'd be down. But he didn't know that. Well, obviously he did, but he wasn't supposed to!

I didn't plan on seeing him at all today. But the entire time I was in Starbucks I was thinking about him. Just like when I first got up this morning and showered. And while I dressed. And while I drove to Starbucks. So I just said fuck it. Maybe if I saw him that would get him out of my head.

But seeing him didn't help.

That actually made it worse.

Then he was being all… take charge and controlly with his sexy ass. Those lips. Those eyes. Ugh. I just feel so helpless when I'm in his presence. Even without him saying a word to me… it's like… he speaks to me. I don't know.

So yea, I dropped the coffee and banana bread off or whatever and went back to my crib, but then I remembered that I didn't have to sleep the day away since I didn't have to go to the strip club tonight. I decided to take me a few days to just rest before I started looking for another job, so I rested a little and did some cleaning and grocery shopping. It was while I put my groceries away that I received back to back calls from an unknown number. I never answer calls I don't know, and I started not to answer this time as well, but something inside of me told me to answer. And I did. And it was Hunter telling me that he had been arrested at work and needed me to come and bail him out.

He was telling me that he'd be able to pay me back as soon as he was out and all of that bullshit, but at that moment… all I could think about was getting him out because I knew he was there because of me. Why else would he have gotten arrested? That creepy ass nigga that tried to get one over on me had to press charges because he got his ass whooped.

After I paid for his bail, I made my way to 201, and this is what I walk into. Him being hounded by his parents… mostly his mother… with a look on his face that I'd never seen before. A look that I didn't like on him at all. I didn't want to be all in their business, so I nodded at him and turned to walk out figuring he was going to leave with them, but he called my name and stopped me.

I turned around and smiled at the sight of him doing a slight jog towards me.

"Hey," he mumbled when he stood in front of me. "Thanks for coming."

"Hey. What happened?"

"Assault charge. From last night."

"Shit. I knew it. I'm so sorry, Hunter. Don't even worry about paying me back, and I'll pay any court costs you may have. My word might not mean much, but I have no problem telling them that you did that to protect me."

"You have nothing to apologize for, Onyx. The police could have been in the gas station standing next to me and I still would've did what I did."

His mother's voice cut my reply off as she made her way behind us.

"I should've known," she started, and his father rolled his eyes and grabbed her hand. "I should have known this had something to do with her. Why are you wasting your time with her, Hunter? Why is she here?" ·

"She's here because I called her. Not you. How did you even know I was here?"

"Michelle called us and told us that you were arrested."

"Michelle had no right to call you and tell you anything. I'll handle that when I get back to work."

"She cares about you, honey. She wants what's best for you. She is who's best for you."

His mother looked at me quickly and stuck her nose so high up I could see the booger that was about to make its way down. The sight made me chuckle during what would have otherwise pissed me clean off.

"Do you need a ride, son?" his father asked.

"Uh." Hunter looked at me for confirmation that I'd take him home and I nodded. "Ima ride with, Onyx."

"You what? Hunter, if you don't get your narrow behind…"

His father pulled his mother away from us and Hunter shook his head as he grabbed my hand and led me out of the precinct. We walked to my car in silence. I let him drive. And after we'd made it like a mile away from the precinct he looked over at me and sighed.

"Sorry about my ma. She trips a lot."

I shrugged and looked out of my window. Trying desperately not to question him about who Michelle was and why she felt the need to call his parents on his behalf.

As if he knew what I was thinking he mumbled, "Michelle is a girl that I work with that has a crush on me. My mother has been trying to hook us up since I started working at the station. I have no interest in her whatsoever."

I shrugged again and looked at him briefly before returning my attention to the window.

"You don't have to explain who she is to me, Hunter Hendrix."

But thank the Lawd he did!!!

I wasn't going to let his ass know that, though.

"You don't have to act like you don't care, Onyx Stanford. It's okay to like me, beautiful. I have absolutely no intentions of hiding how I feel about you... or how attracted to you I am."

His hand reached over to my side of the car and grabbed mine, and as much as I wanted to pull it away is as much as I wanted it to stay. I shook my head in disbelief as my eyes watered. Like... I couldn't understand for the life of me why he wanted me or what he wanted from me.

Hunter Hendrix was no standard nigga.

I didn't know much about him... but I knew enough to know that he could have just about any woman he wanted. So why did he want me? His relationship with God seemed to be genuine, so it wasn't for my sex. And because his relationship with God was genuine, I just couldn't understand what he could have possibly wanted with me.

"What do you want from me?" I heard myself ask... and as soon as I did I wanted to take it back. I tried to pull my hand from his but he held it tighter.

"I just want you."

"But why? I'm not your type. I'm not a Christian. I'm a fucking stripper."

"You don't even know my type. I don't consider myself to be a Christian either. Jesus wasn't a Christian. That's who I'm trying to live like. That is my Teacher. I'm a disciple, a student of Christ. That's it. And you *used* to be a stripper. You're not anymore."

"You're right, I don't know your type, but I can pretty much guarantee you it ain't me."

"Just… give me the time and chance tonight to show you how wrong you are."

"Your mother doesn't like me. She'll probably never like me."

Why did that matter? Why did I care? It wasn't like we were getting married or no shit like that.

"I didn't think you'd be the type to care about what anyone thought about you."

"I'm not."

"So why does it matter what my mother thinks about you?"

"It doesn't."

"Good. Besides… she doesn't know you anyway. And she's not the one trying to build with you. I am."

"But why?"

He shrugged and ran his thumb against my hand.

"I could tell you, and you'd end up questioning it. Or I could just show you, and force you to believe it with my actions. Which do you prefer?"

"Both."

He smiled, which made me smile, and I found myself leaning to the left just to be a little closer to him.

"You asked me what do I want from you? I do want you, but I guess there are some things I would need from you if we ever took things to the next level."

"And what would you need from me, Hunter?"

"I need you to respect me. Love me. Submit to me and let me lead you as your man. Grace me with your feminine energy by doing the things I absolutely can't or won't. Like after we're married give me babies…"

"Hold up. Babies? Married? We haven't even gone out on a date yet."

"Cause you playing."

"How am I playing?"

He looked over at me briefly and smiled.

"You're not ready yet, Onyx. Just trust me and enjoy the ride, baby."

"Fine. Can you at least tell me why me?"

"I could… but you wouldn't believe me. Ask God."

Okay. Like. The hell was I supposed to say to that shit? Me and God ain't cool like that for Him to be talking to me. I mean… I pray and I talk to Him, but I swear sometimes it feels like a one sided conversation. I guess in a sense He talks to me through His word, but I be needing guidance and confirmation that I can actually hear.

So, instead of going back and forth with Hunter's roundabout ass I just returned my attention to the window. And the rest of our ride was done in silence.

Hunter

It was no surprise to me that my mother summoned my presence when I got off work. She would have a million questions about why I was arrested, why I didn't call her, and why Onyx was there. A nigga really wasn't in the mood to be questioned, but I knew that if I didn't go ahead and get it out the way that she would show up at my place. So, when I got off I made my way straight to my parents' home to get my interrogation out of the way.

For a few minutes, I just... sat in my car and prayed before I even went in. Prayed for strength. The strength to hold my tongue and remain respectful. My mother had a way of getting under my skin like no one else could. She swore it was out of love, and in a sense it was, but it was also out of a need to control my life.

I'd quickly gotten a rep as the rebellious son, so she went above and beyond in my younger days trying to keep me down the path she wanted me to take. That only made me rebel even harder. Now... our relationship was... weird. I loved and respected her with all that was in me, with all of the God that was in me. I just... didn't like her very much.

That didn't mean I wouldn't lay down my life for her. And I'd give her anything she wanted and needed. But if I could do that from a distance... I would.

I sluggishly made my way to their front door, and I hadn't rang the doorbell good before my pops was opening it and stepping outside quickly.

"Son..." he mumbled while looking behind him as if my mother could see through the door.

I chuckled and took a step back with a shake of my head. You know that part in the bible that talks about it being better to live in the dessert than with a quarrelsome and nagging wife... yea... that was my pops. But he loved and accepted my mother, though. And I respected him so much for that.

"What's up, Pops?"

"I just wanted to warn you before you went in there."

"Warn me about what?"

He grabbed my forearm and pulled me further away from the door.

"Two months ago... Pastor Stanford asked your mother and I to meet with him."

"...Oookay?"

"About you. And Onyx."

"Me and Onyx? What about me and Onyx? I didn't even know her two months ago. Well, I knew her, but I hadn't met her yet."

"Basically... he thinks you're the key to getting her saved and back in the church. She's his next in line, and he wants that to be fulfilled through you."

I took two steps back and eyed him skeptically.

"Next in line for what?"

My pops chuckled… but I didn't see a thang that was funny! I was cool with sitting on a middle pew during service. Being a Pastor wasn't even the last thing on my mind. I didn't want that responsibility. I didn't want that weight on my shoulders. That judgment. That pressure. No. No thank you.

"To lead his church, Hunter. He wants you to take his place when he steps down."

"Why me? Doesn't that spot automatically go to someone of the Stanford bloodline?"

"Yes. By blood. Or marriage. It will go to Onyx by blood. You by marriage."

I lifted my hands and shook my head as I took a few more steps back. Yea… there was definitely something about Onyx that I'd been drawn to since the first night I saw her. And there was a tug at my spirit that told me that she was my rib. But this…

"Why me?"

I found myself laughing quietly at the thought of Onyx asking me the exact same thing earlier today.

"I don't know, son. You'll have to take that up with Pastor Stanford and God. He did say something to the extent of needing a certain kind of man to pull Onyx back in and you being it."

My inhale was hard and deep as millions of thoughts rushed my brain.

"I'm down for doing all that I can to help Onyx. To be honest…

I could even see myself being with Onyx. But being the head of his or anyone else's church is just not what I had in mind for my life."

His hand cupped my shoulder firmly.

"That's fine, son. It doesn't have to be. Just remember Proverbs 16:9."

And with that... he walked away. I followed behind slowly as I tried to remember Proverbs 16:9. All of the different translations I'd read over the years were blurring my memory, but it was something to the extent of... a man's heart and / or mind can make their plans, but the Lord guides his steps.

Onyx

My relationship with my parents' was… distant to say the least. There were no random visits and hour long conversations. We didn't get together for holidays. Well… they did with my family… but I wasn't there. My father texted me every morning and told me that he loved me. My mom called me once or twice a week just to hear my voice. My grandparents and I hadn't spoken in years.

And all of my cousins for the most part were so scared to disappoint my grandparents that they lived life with façades. And I hate liars. Even those who live life as a liar. So we didn't kick it. My cousins that chose to take their own paths moved out of Memphis completely. We talk every once in a while, and I visit them when I need a break. But for the most part… it's always been… just me.

The fact that my mother randomly popped up at my spot and rung my doorbell had me feeling some type of way. My first thought was that someone was dead. It's a shame when the only time your family gets together is at a funeral.

I hadn't seen my mother in about nine months, so when I opened the door and saw an older version of me standing on the other side… it took me a minute to process it. When I was able to process it, I let her in and she made her way to my kitchen for a cup of hot tea.

Now, we were sitting here in this awkward ass silence. Looking everywhere but at each other. Her fingers were drumming the side of her cup while mine did the same thing on top of the table. I looked at the time on top of my stove and shook my head. I needed to get ready for my date with Hunter Hendrix. My date with Hunter Hendrix. My first *real* date. Sure, my sugar daddies took me out, but I'd never considered those to be dates.

And to think… my first date… out of my whole twenty-six years of life is with someone as fine, and deep, and strong, and complex yet simple as…

"I came over to talk to you about Hunter. Shantel, his mother, she called me earlier and had quite a bit to say."

My top lip twisted up as I sat back in my seat. Figures. She would stop by because of something someone in the church said to her. I scratched my neck and tilted my head as I waited for her to continue.

"She was rattling on about Hunter being arrested and her thinking it had something to do with you. She said she hadn't talked to him about it yet, but that she wanted me to warn you to stay away from him. Shantel seems to have someone in mind for Hunter, and she doesn't want you negatively influencing him or standing in the way of that."

My smile was not a happy one. It was one that was filled with disbelief, yet strangely this was exactly what I expected from her.

"Ma…"

"Before you go into telling me your side of the story, first let me tell you that Shantel is *not* someone whose word I would believe over yours. The only reason I said that is because I promised her that I would relay the message before she even told me what it was.

I don't know enough about the situation to agree with her, or say anything to you about being right or wrong, so don't be defensive, Gem."

This time, when I smiled it was genuine. She and my father never called me Onyx. They always called me Gem. She said that's what she originally wanted to name me, but she chose Onyx because my father said it held more power.

"Hunter was arrested because of me. The night before last, this guy came into the… he came where I was and tried to… you know. I fought him off but Hunter saw some blood and questioned me about it. Yesterday, Hunter confronted the guy. He was arrested for the assault. I didn't ask him to do anything, he did it on his own. But I told him that I'd pay whatever court costs he may have, even though I have a feeling he won't let me, and that I was willing to give a statement on his behalf."

"Gem…" My mother sat up in her seat with the most distressed look on her face. "Are you telling me a man tried to rape you?"

I nodded and slid further down in my seat.

"Did you file a police report?"

"File a police report? For what? For them to tell me that they don't have enough evidence and it's his word over mine? That he's more believable because of my occupation?"

"So… this has happened before?"

I shrugged and crossed my arms over my chest. It had. That's why I started carrying my knife on me and my gun in my car. I wasn't going to tell her that and have her worrying even more about me, though.

"It's not that big of a deal, Ma, really. Hunter..." I couldn't help but smile just at the mention of his name. "He was there for me in a major way. A way I didn't even realize I needed someone to be. So... I'm fine."

"You're not fine, Gem. You need to stop with this... this... foolishness. You have your degree in Art History. You're a beautiful, intelligent, and creative young lady. When are you going to let go of what happened or didn't happen in your childhood and move on?"

Was she serious right now? Like... seriously? Like... she expects me to just... let go of what happened or didn't happen in my childhood? If she can't even acknowledge it, how in the hell does she expect me to dig it up just to bury it?

"You know what, Ma, I have to get ready to go out in a few. So... if that's all..."

I refused to tell her that I wasn't stripping anymore. She'd just pissed me clean off. It was always this with them. Like my childhood was the way it was because of me. Like I chose to alienate myself from them. Like it was as easy as simply flipping a switch and every negative feeling I've ever felt about myself that made me believe I was unlovable and unwanted would just go away.

"That's... that's not all, baby. I'm sorry. I know you're sensitive about that. I'm sorry. It's just... I worry about you so much. I really wish you would just stop."

When she realized I wasn't going to respond to that she continued.

"I actually... I'm so happy that you and Hunter found each other. He's literally an answered prayer that I've been praying for years for you. I don't know the extent of your friendship or relationship with him… but… he's a really great guy, Gem.

I've been praying that God would send you your Adam. Not another man to use and abuse the tortured child within you. But your Adam. And I believe Hunter is it."

"What do you mean my Adam?"

"People think that when God said it wasn't good for man to be alone that he meant all men, but that's not true. It's a certain type of man that's worthy of the love, submission, and companionship that comes from a woman.

Women are nurturers and adapters naturally. We're incubators. We naturally give birth to whatever seeds a man give us. Whether it be his literal seed for us to give birth to children… or seeds of love, seeds of unhappiness, seeds of his vision that we help him manifest. Whatever the case may be. Anything a man gives a woman she gives back multiplied.

Now, when God said that it wasn't good for man to be alone… there were five things that He'd set in place for Adam before He made that realization.

He placed Adam in the garden of Eden. Meaning he brought Adam into his presence. Adam had a relationship with God. He gave Adam work and responsibility. He gave him the responsibility of keeping and cultivating the garden as its worker and protector. And He gave Adam His word and command.

After all of this, God said that it wasn't good for man to be alone. The man that it isn't good for him to be alone is a man that spends time in the presence of God. A man who works and can provide for his family. A man who can cultivate his woman and make her better. Produce fruit with her. Keep and protect her and their union together. And he has to know the word of God so he can lead his woman.

That's the kind of man that deserves a wife. And that's the kind of man Hunter is."

How did she know what kind of man Hunter was? I mean... okay... so... he did have a relationship with God. He does have a solid career. He does seem like he's invested in cultivating me and making me better. He definitely has proven himself to be my protector. And he knows the word of God.

Humph.

"He might be all of that, but who's to say that he wants that with me? We just started engaging with each other. I will admit, he has definitely had a positive impact on my life since he's been in it, but I don't want to rush this, Ma."

"Gem, if Hunter didn't want that with you, Shantel wouldn't have called me. Obviously there is something there if she sees you as a threat to whoever she wants for him."

"Michelle," I mumbled before I could catch myself.

"Michelle, huh? She must not go to the church?"

"She works with him."

She nodded with a small smile.

"Well, all I can say, baby, is to explore this with all that you have. Even if it doesn't lead to marriage, although I'm praying it will, I definitely believe it will be good for you."

As much as I didn't want to admit it, I did too.

"Yea, well, he's actually taking me out tonight so..."

"Is he? Great! I'm going to head on out and let you get ready."

She jumped from her seat so quickly it made me chuckle. Surprisingly, she made her way around the table and placed a soft kiss on my cheek.

"I love you, Gem."

I was so caught off guard all I could do was nod. It wasn't until she'd walked out of the kitchen that I found the voice to say...

"I love you too."

-&-

I wasn't sure where we going or what we were doing, so I had absolutely no idea how to dress. The past two hours of my life had been spent pulling literally every article of clothing I owned out and tossing it on my bed. And when my doorbell rang... oh my God... my heart felt like it was about to burst out of my rib cage into little strings of confetti. Where had the freaking time gone?!

I still had to do my hair and makeup. I had no idea what I was going to wear. And here he was. At my door. All on time and shit. Actually, he was five minutes early. And I started to throw a fit about that, but there wasn't much I could've done in five minutes to get ready anyway. When I opened the door and saw him standing on the other side...

He was standing there looking all good with his freshly cut

tapered fade. He had diamonds in both ears. His beard was neatly trimmed as it had been every time I saw him. Those lips... he licked those full pink brown lips as he looked me up and down and all it took all the self-control I had to not suck the bottom one into my mouth.

"Um... I take it you need a minute to finish getting ready?" he asked.

I looked into his beautiful brown eyes briefly before taking in the rest of his body. Hunter had the type of body that looked as if he worked out... but his muscles weren't excessive.

"Yea, I... I can't find anything to wear."

"Okay. Let me pick."

Without waiting for an invitation, Hunter Hendrix made his way down my hall like he knew where he was going. I shook my head and chuckled as he looked in every room until he found my bedroom.

For a second I just stood there and took in the fact that he looked and smelled so damn good. How was I supposed to get through the night without begging him to touch me? Kiss me? Hell, at this point, I'd settle from him getting close enough for me to feel his breath on me. Let his cologne embed itself in my skin so I can feel him and smell him after he leaves.

"Lawd have mercy," I heard him say from my room.

And that's when I remembered that it looked a hot damn mess! Who the hell just walks into somebody's spot and goes into their room without permission? Hunter Hendrix. I walked back to my room and saw him flipping through different pieces of clothing that were on my bed.

"Onyx..."

"Didn't nobody tell you to be all up in my room, Hunter Hendrix. It's... usually... clean. I just... I told you I couldn't find anything to wear."

His smile made me feel a little less defensive, so I walked towards him and gave myself the pleasure of inhaling his cologne again. Would it have been weird if I just wrapped my arms around him from behind and pressed my nose into his back so I could get closer? Smell him better? Let it hit me deeper?

Probably so.

He already probably thinks I'm crazy.

I shouldn't do that.

Hunter turned to face me and I pulled my arms behind my back to keep from touching him.

"Huh." I looked down at his extended arm as he tried to hand me a one-piece jumpsuit. "Put this on."

"But it's black."

He was dressed in a black v neck that fit him so perfectly I could see the lining of his muscles and six pack. I didn't want to do the corny same color couple thing. Because... because I'd fall for him even more and gush over how good we looked together all night. And want to take pictures. And put them on social media. And tag him as my #MCE. And... that... just... could not happen. It would not happen. I refused to let it happen.

"So?"

"So? You have on black."

Hunter shrugged and pushed the suit into my chest. I grabbed it and he began to walk out immediately. With a groan and roll of my eyes I headed for my bathroom to shower. This nigga.

Hunter

Onyx was beautiful when she let me inside of her home, but she wasn't dressed. And the last thing I needed was time alone with her at this point. I guess you could say we were at that infatuation stage of knowing each other. All I wanted to do was lay up with her and look at her and touch on her, and all she wanted to do was deny how she felt about me because she liked me so much. And she hated liking me so much.

I messed myself up with the outfit I picked for her, though. Two hours after I arrived she walked into her living room looking like… a goddess. Looking like… the woman I wanted to spend the rest of my life with. Looking like… the woman I wanted to have on my arm everywhere I went.

Her scent caught my attention first. Whatever perfume she had on was sweet. Fruity. Edible. Had me looking up and licking my lips. It ain't no secret, women are stimulated by what they hear. Men by what they see. And I hadn't been able to keep my eyes off of her since she we left her house.

The one piece that she had on was black, and it fit her body so perfectly that it looked like her skin. Every curve on her body was put on display. The top of it was sheer with black lace flowers covering her breasts, the sides of her stomach, her shoulders, and the sides of her back. Her arms, the middle of her stomach and chest, and the sides of her breasts were visible because of the sheer material. And had I known it was going to look like that I wouldn't have picked it.

The last thing I wanted to do was put myself in the position to not be able to function around her from lusting after her so much. It wasn't her fault that she looked so good. It was my responsibility to keep my self-control and not lead us down a path that would most certainly lead to sex.

Onyx had on some light makeup, and she had her real hair pulled up into a sleek bun, thank the Lord. I hated when she had that green wig on. It wasn't ugly or ratchet looking or anything like that. I just... liked the real her better.

I took her to Itta Bena for dinner, then we went across the block to listen to some live blues music and get our little two step in. Which apparently surprised her because she looked like I'd asked her to kill a nigga for me when I asked her to dance. Like, because I was in tune with the God in me that I didn't dance or listen to anything other than Gospel music.

When she realized that I was just a normal man with a little bit of a glow about himself, she loosened up and became her true self with me. We danced for hours. We danced until her feet hurt. And I can honestly say I've never seen a sight more beautiful than that of Onyx Stanford laughing and having a good time.

I led her to an empty corner in the back of the lounge and pulled her feet up into my lap. After I took the heels that she was wearing off and began to massage her foot she said...

"Tell me about you, Hunter Hendrix."

Her interest in me caught me off guard, so I stopped massaging her foot, but I quickly recovered and continued before I spoke.

"What do you want to know?"

"Everything."

I started to not tell her about my pre-Christ life, but I figured that would better help her understand why I understood her. To be honest, I've had my fair share of judgment from people at church and that I work with as well. So I completely understood the fact that she removed herself from the church to avoid that judgment and hypocrisy. It was like… some people in the church… they couldn't see their own sin because they were focused on others. And just because someone's sin wasn't the same as theirs… it made them feel like they were better, or even just that that person was worse.

It took me learning for myself that we all have struggles, and no one is perfect, not even those that claim to be, for me to be able to stay in the church. I had to learn not to punish God and rob myself of Him and eternity with Him because of what people who claim to serve Him say and do.

Onyx would get to that point too. She would definitely get to that point too.

"Well, you know my name. I'm twenty-eight years old. The youngest of three boys. My parents are Carlton and Shantel Hendrix. Completely single and unattached. No ex-wives or baby mama's. No ex-girlfriends sticking around on the friend tip. The only person you'll ever have to worry about coming before you if we ever got serious is

God. Other than that, you would always come first with me, Onyx."

I don't know why I felt it in my spirit to assure her of that, but I did, and when I did… she inhaled deeply as her eyes watered. Yea, she'd told me about feeling alone and unloved and unwanted, but I thought that that was something she'd grown out of. I guess not. After making the mental note to shower her with as much love and attention and affection as I possibly could from this point forward I continued.

"Uh… I had a decent childhood. Fought a lot. Smoked and sold weed. Gang banger."

"Woah, woah, hold up. Wait."

Onyx lifted her hands and removed her feet from my lap so she could sit straight up to look at me. I smiled with half of my mouth as I lowered my head and ran my hand over my hair.

"Say what now?"

"I told you I ain't been saved all my life."

"Well… yea… but damn. I wasn't expecting that. You got some bar time behind you?"

"Yep. Convicted of manslaughter when I was fifteen. Did seven years."

"Damn."

"Yep. Got out when I was twenty-two. Got my relationship with God right, and that led to getting my life right. Went to TSU and graduated with a degree in broadcasting. Now I'm the head of our media department at church, and I'm on the production team at Fox 13. You know that. I do video and film production and directing on the side as well."

"That explains it," she mumbled so softly I hardly heard her.

"Explains what?"

Her eyes and head lowered, and she tried to move away from me slightly, but I wrapped my arm around her waist and kept her close.

"Explains what, Onyx?"

"Why you're not the average church boy."

"Yea, there is definitely nothing about me that is average." She smiled and turned towards the right... scooting a little closer to me. "Now tell me about you."

"You know about me."

"I don't know about you. I knew about what you used to do. Not you."

She bit down on her lip as I took her hand into mine.

"Okay. Um... you know my parents. See them more than me. I'm the only child. Twenty-six. Currently unemployed because someone made me quit my job." She chuckled, and I couldn't help but laugh myself and shake my head. "Graduated with a degree in Art History."

"Really?"

Onyx nodded and blushed innocently.

"Yea. I dig art. Like... if I've ever loved anything that'd be it."

"That explains the tattoos, piercings, and green hair. Why aren't you using your degree, Onyx?"

She shrugged as she looked out into the distance.

"I don't know. Just… got side tracked I guess, but… since I have the time I'm going to do some research and make sure that my next job is actually a career in my field."

"What are some things you could do with that degree besides teach and work at a museum?"

"Well… I could open my own art gallery. Work as an appraiser or art and antique dealer. I could be an art buyer… but I don't think I'd have any luck finding something like in Memphis."

"You don't need luck when you have grace."

We locked eyes until she got chills. Literal chills. Her hands ran up and down her arms, and I looked. And that's what I saw. Chill bumps.

"What do you like to do in your free time?" She asked.

"Chill. I rip and run so much because of church and my job and the side jobs I do that when I have the time I just… chill. Kick it at the house. Have me a drink or two. Watch a game. Listen to music."

"Have a drink or two? Of liquor?"

I smiled as her thumb ran across my hand.

"Yes, Onyx. I don't get drunk. I'm not addicted. I drink it modestly in the comfort of my own home. I don't order wine or a beer when I'm out with other Christians because I don't want to offend them and make them stumble in their walk by judging me.

But I do have the occasional drink every once in a while."

"See, had I met you before I left the church… someone who was genuine… I probably wouldn't have left. I've always believed what mattered most was your relationship with God and your spiritual condition. What you exude spiritually. The condition of your heart and mind. Not what you eat, drink, and wear.

But my parents… they were so old school they picked at every little thing I said and did, you know?"

"Yea that's, that's that old school new wine in old wineskins mentality. Their parents got it from their parents who got it from their parents and it has been passed down from generation to generation without any real thought or study from one's self. That's just like with tattoos. People use the same scripture to condemn people with tattoos without taking the time to actually study the history and context of that passage.

Most of my friends aren't Christians, and the ones that are saved were saved under me because I showed them a different view of Jesus. A more genuine view of Jesus."

"That makes perfect sense. Jesus spent most of his time with sinners outside of church. Most of his ministry was done in the streets. He didn't reach people with judgment and condemnation. He did it with love. There is a lack of love these days, man."

"I completely agree. We should spend more time loving and accepting people and inviting them to come as they are. That way God will have room to speak to their hearts. But if their hearts are closed to him because of things we say and do we'll end up doing more harm than good. No souls will be saved. No hearts will be reached. No minds will be changed. And the only people that'll make it to heaven are the ones in the church."

"And probably half of them won't even make it in. You'd be

surprised how many secrets I found out about as a little girl through my grandpops. When he prayed for his members he actually spoke it and called them out by name. And my nosey ass was up listening instead of sleeping. So many people lying and cheating. Dealing with porn addictions and homosexuality. And those same people would be in the choir Sunday, or at the church picnic clowning somebody else.

I don't know why that bothered me so much… but it really irritated me to my soul."

"It's because you have a genuine spirit. When you have a genuine spirit liars and frauds disturb you. You either expect everyone to be just as genuine as you, or you allow your disappointments from those who aren't to keep you guarded and closed off from people because you fear no one is as genuine as you."

Her head tilted, and her eyes landed on my lips. She wanted me to kiss her. I wanted to kiss her. But since I wasn't sure that's where I'd be able to stop, I resisted.

"It's getting late, baby. We should probably head back in."

"K," she whispered as she placed her feet back inside of her shoes.

I felt bad. I felt like… like she needed this. Like she needed me. Like she needed to feel wanted. And as much as I wanted to make her feel wanted, I had to keep myself from taking things too far. Onyx stood. So did I. She tried to walk away, but I grabbed her forearm and pulled her closer to me. Her lips were so full. They looked so soft. Like they would connect with mine perfectly.

It seemed like anytime I was around her I couldn't help but touch her in some way. From something as simple as touching her hair to holding her hand. Now was no different. I cupped her cheek and caressed it with my thumb.

"I really want to kiss you," I told her.

"Then kiss me."

"But I don't want to make this harder than it already is."

Onyx smiled as she wrapped her arms around my neck. I wrapped mine around her waist.

"It's definitely hard."

I chuckled and tried to put some space between us so she wouldn't be able to feel the effect she had on me, but she wouldn't let me.

"Hunter, I have no intentions of making you fall because of me. I know you don't want to have sex until you're married. As much as I want to take it there with you, I have no problem waiting. I'm enjoying this that we have. It's… something I've never experienced with anyone else. I can get sex from anyone. But I can't get from anyone what I'm getting from you."

"But I don't want you getting it from anyone else either."

"I don't want it from anyone else. If I'm not getting it from you… I just won't get it."

I inhaled deeply and nodded as I continued to stare at her. She was taking this no sex thing better than I thought she would. It wasn't about premarital sex being a sin. It wasn't about the possibility of contracting STD's and HIV. It wasn't even about getting a woman pregnant.

The older I get… the wiser I get. The more differently I see things. The better I understand things. And one of the best lessons that I've learned is that sex bonds people together in a way that nothing else can. Soul ties are real. When a woman is in tune with her feminine energy, sex to her is an act of trust. She's giving herself to a man because she sees a future with him.

She's giving him pieces of her that should be reserved for her husband. The only man really guaranteed to give her all that she wants and needs. And I just ain't the type of nigga to take things that don't belong to me.

I don't need the drama of a female being attached to me because we're having sex and she's expecting commitment, marriage, and kids. I don't need the guilt of hurting a woman because it's over and she has to start over again. With yet another man. Hoping he'll be the one.

So, when I chose to practice celibacy years ago it was because of how much I valued women and their hearts, how worthy I knew they were. And I just... wasn't trying to go back on that now.

But even with all of that... I still wanted to kiss her.

Onyx

Last night... I could tell Hunter wanted to kiss me. It was cute how hard he was fighting his desire for me. On the ride home, he kept looking over at me shaking his head. Like he was disappointed in himself. Like he couldn't believe he didn't take advantage of the opportunity to take it there with me.

I understood his reasoning, and I agreed. For once... I didn't want a man's money or sex. I wanted things from Hunter that I didn't know I was capable of getting.

Love.

Respect.

Time and attention.

Affection.

I just... want somebody that's going to treat me like somebody. Like I matter. I want a man that sees me and only me. A man that adores me. A man that chooses me to experience things with him in life that he won't experience with anyone else. Like marriage. And parenthood. And love for eternity. And Hunter... I believe Hunter is that man. Because of that, there's nothing I'm willing to do to jeopardize what we're building.

He came in last night, and we talked some more. And some more.

And some more. We ended up falling asleep together on my couch. When I woke up it was around four in the morning. I was laying on his chest, and his arms were wrapped around me. The second I tried to get up he held me tighter. So, I just… went back to sleep.

The next time I woke up it was with the rising of the sun. His fingers were running up and down my back and against my cheek. And the shit put me right back to sleep.

Then, I woke up around nine. Alone. All except for a handwritten note from him. A note that said he hated to leave, especially with me looking so beautiful in my sleep, and he was going to quickly make his way back to me.

After I showered and ate breakfast, I decided to hit the ground running with the whole finding a career thing. After talking to Hunter about finishing school and not doing anything with my degree, I kind of got excited about finally stepping into my field.

For years I made the monthly payment on a storage unit that housed all of the paintings I'd purchased and painted since I was thirteen. After doing an online search and filling out a few applications, I went to the storage unit and picked up a few of the pieces I painted and took them home. Then, I went to Michael's and grabbed a few sketchpads, canvas pads, and a new set of Acrylic paints.

When I made it home I ate again and lost myself in painting. It had been years since I painted or sketched anything, and it wasn't until my doorbell rang and I pulled myself away from the canvas painting that I realized I'd been at it for hours.

My mind was so into what I was doing that I paid no attention to my appearance, or put any thought to who could have been on the other side of my door. But the sight of Hunter immediately pulled me out of my creative flow and brought me back to reality. I looked from the gorgeous smile that was plastered on his face, to the large white t-shirt covered in splattered paint that I wore. My hand went to the top of my head, and I ran my fingers through my wavy armpit length hair.

Anytime I painted I wanted to be as free as I possibly could. The less clothing the better. I wanted nothing restricting me. Not even a ponytail holder.

His thumb ran across my cheek and he smiled harder.

"Beloved, you have never looked more beautiful than you do right now."

I blushed and opened the door wider for him to enter.

"I look a mess," I replied as I closed and locked the door behind him.

"You look like your purpose."

"Hunter…"

He pulled me into him by my waist and kissed my lips so soft and quickly that I wouldn't have known his lips were there had mine not trembled from the contact.

"I love this," he mumbled into my lips as his hands slid through my disheveled hair.

"Hun…"

His lips pressed into mine with more pressure this time, and I couldn't help but moan and submit as he used his tongue to open my mouth. I don't know what I expected kissing a church boy to be like… but kissing Hunter was not it. There was nothing godly about the way he kissed me. He kissed me with straight up passion. Heat. Lust. Rawness.

With each slow swirl of his tongue around mine. Each pull of my lips into his mouth. Each bite. Each lick. Each suck. Each low groan and whisper that seeped from his lips. Maybe it was God. Maybe it was something that was holy and set apart, because I had never ever experienced anything like that before.

When he finally pulled his lips from mine, I didn't open my eyes right away. I let the feel of his lips linger on mine. I licked the remnants of him from my mouth before opening my eyes slowly. When I did, I smiled immediately at the sight of brown paint on his cheek.

"You have paint on you," I mumbled, then realized I had paint on me. "Shit." I tried to walk away to clean myself, but he grabbed my wrist and pulled me back into him.

It only took me three seconds of staring into his eyes before paint and my appearance weren't even the last things on my mind.

"Onyx…" My eyes closed immediately at the sound of my name. He'd said my name before. I'd heard my name millions of times before. But it was something about the way he said it then that just… shook me. He said my name like… like it was his. Like I was his. Like I belonged to him. "I want to know you in every way possible. I want to know everything about you that there is to know. Don't deny me of that."

"I won't," I answered more quickly than I ever had before.

"You know what you have to do."

I did. The answer wasn't in my mind. It was in my heart. If I wanted to experience all that I could with Hunter, I had to get me together. I had to get my shit together. Soon.

"I'm not ready," I replied honestly.

There were so many skeletons in my closet. So many things I had to let go of to make room for his love. But the thought of cleaning out my closet was just as draining as the actual process would probably be.

"I'll be with you every step of the way. My love won't mean anything to you if you aren't open to receive it. And you can't receive it holding on to all you're holding on to. All I wanna do is love you, Onyx. That's it."

For the first time, I didn't question him. I didn't seek to be pacified by words that in the back of my mind I wouldn't be able to conceive as true. I didn't doubt his attraction and attachment to me. I didn't allow my past to make me feel unworthy of him and all that he wanted to offer me.

For the first time, I didn't need to know how everything would play out. I didn't know what would be the Alpha and Omega, the beginning and the end of us. I didn't need him to assure me that he was telling the truth.

I was willing to allow him to prove that this that was happening between us went beyond us. That I didn't have to know everything. That we didn't have to have answers to everything. That our vibe was enough. That our chemistry was enough. That the tug in my heart every time I was in his presence was enough. That his desire for me was enough. That him seeing me and looking beyond my flaws was enough.

He looked beyond my flaws.

He looked beyond my flaws in the way I imagined God could. God would. If I let him.

He looked beyond my past and chose to love me in spite of me.

He looked beyond my past and chose to love me in spite of me in the way I imagined God could. God would. If I let him.

This shit was… way too fucking much. I took a step away from him, yet felt compelled to draw closer to him.

"You're beautiful," he uttered softly. "Baby, if I could explain why I feel the way I do for you I would, but there's no other way for me to describe it other than saying it's unconditional. It really has nothing to do with you. All I wanna do is shower you with the love of God. I've given myself to Him for His use. I've opened myself up to Him, and I'm allowing Him to love you through me. I wish I could tell you an exact thing you said or did, or a moment where I decided to commit myself to this… to you… but I can't. All I can do is say what's in my heart. And that is the fact that just as God looks beyond your flaws and your past… so will I."

I broke out into a sob that turned into a laugh before returning to a sob.

"Why did you have to say that?"

He took my hand into his and pulled me back into him slowly. His hand cupped my cheeks, and I looked into his eyes. His piercing eyes. I swear it felt like he was looking right into my soul.

"He doesn't see what you see," Hunter muttered as he caressed my cheeks with his thumbs. "And I don't either. I don't see your spots. Your wrinkles. Your blemishes. We think you're beautiful. That you're marvelous. And you're worth... so much more than a few coins and designer labels, Onyx. Let us give you that."

I was tired. Tired of running. Tired of hiding. Tired of holding back and in what I desperately needed to let go of. Tired of settling. For once, for fucking once, I wanted to take a chance on something that was good for my soul. So...

"I don't know what this will lead to, and I'm scared as hell, Hunter, but I want this. I want you. I... I want Him. But I'm not perfect and I probably won't ever be. I..."

His pointing finger on my lips silenced me.

"Neither of us expect you to be. God is the only being that can be or love perfectly. All I ask is that you be genuine, honest, and that you communicate with me so that we always remain on the same page."

"I can do that."

Hunter smiled, before kissing my nose softly.

"So... are you like... my boyfriend?"

His smile widened as I wrapped my arms around his waist.

"That depends. I'm kind of a package deal. If you want me, you have to be okay with God being the foundation we stand on. Marriage is a God thing, so I can't enter into a union without Him and expect Him to bless it."

"Well... what would that mean for us? Would you expect me to change? Stop cursing and smoking and shit because I can't say that I will anytime soon."

"Not at all. I will never try to change you. The only thing that truly changes a person is their desire to change. The only thing that I can do to persuade you is love you and show you how much of a masterpiece you are. If that leads you to want to change some of your habits and lifestyle that's fine. But that's not what I'm about.

When I say God will be our foundation I mean He will be in the center of everything I do. All decisions I make concerning us will be made after prayer and seeking His guidance. You know we won't have sex until we're married. I'll be the man and do all that is expected of me. I will provide. Protect. Love. Lead. Cultivate. But I need you to respect. Submit. Appreciate. Help us both bring our visions to fruition. And give me babies."

"I'm down with that."

I bit down on my lip and stifled a moan as his hands cupped my ass and he pulled me tighter against him. For some reason, maybe the size of his dick and the way he handled me, made us not having sex until we married a nonfactor. There was no doubt in my mind that he would be able to satisfy me physically. There was something about our exchange that let me know that it wouldn't just be something physical.

I felt like we'd be on some other realm shit. Like he would be stroking my heart, mind, body, soul, and spirit all at the same damn time.

And if he used his lips and tongue on my clit the way he'd just kissed me…

"Well, I guess we're really doing this, huh? I'm your man?"

I smiled harder than I ever thought I had before as I buried my head into his chest.

"Yes, Hunter. You're my man."

Hunter

When I left Onyx's place last night it was with the finished product of what she was working on when I arrived. A painting of me. No one had ever done something so... I don't even know. How do you explain that? She said that when she started painting she didn't know what she coming up with. That she just started painting and it turned into a portrait of me.

The second I set my eyes on the painting it filled me with a sense of belonging. It made me feel like I was hers. And she appreciated and cherished and adored me. I've never been the mushy type... but that feeling was greater than any feeling I've ever felt.

I didn't want to leave her last night, but I messed around and spent the night the last time I was there and I didn't want to make that a habit. When you start giving a man husband privileges it takes him even longer to marry you, and I didn't want to get too comfortable and put Onyx in the position to have to wait for me longer than she deserved to.

I took one last look at the painting before grabbing my wallet, phone, and keys to head out for work. Just as I was opening the door, Pastor Stanford was getting ready to knock. He hadn't been to my place since him and a few other men at the church helped me move in, so I figured he was stopping by to talk to me about something serious.

"Pastor Stanford? Is everything alright?"

I moved to the side slightly so he could come in.

"Everything is fine, son. I just wanted to stop by and talk to you before you went to work. Oliver called and told me that Serena paid Onyx a visit yesterday, so I figured I needed to come and speak with you myself."

He sat in the middle of the couch. I sat in the chair across from it. I cupped my hands together in my lap and tilted my head as I waited for him to speak.

"As you know, when I retire, I will need a successor."

"Brother Oliver?" I offered quickly.

Pastor Stanford smiled and shook his head.

"Eh, no. I had someone a little younger in mind. Someone who would be able to draw a younger crowd into the church. Someone who could reach black men. Young black men. Someone with a past in the streets that they could relate to. Someone who got out of the streets and made something of themselves.

Someone who can go into the hardest neighborhoods in Memphis and get them to see that black people are not to be against black people. That we have been wired this way because of our lack of protection. But that we are stronger in unity. And when we stand together there is nothing we can't do."

"I…" I shook my head and leaned back in my seat. "I don't know anyone like that."

"I do."

"Who?"

"You."

"Pastor Stanford..."

"Hear me out. I'm not going to sit here and say the Lord literally spoke to me and said that it was time for me to retire and that you were my replacement. What I will tell you is that for a month straight I had the same dream about retiring and spending the rest of my days traveling with my wife.

For the next month I fasted and prayed and asked the Lord consistently who he wanted to replace me. I told him that I needed a sign. I needed him to show me exactly who he wanted to replace me. I asked him to make it clear and to give me peace with His decision.

I told him to have whoever my replacement was to call me that day and tell me that the Lord placed it in their heart to call and check on me. Not less than ten minutes later... you called. And do you know what you said? You said that you were praying and my name dropped into your spirit, and you took that as a sign to call and check on me."

I ran my hands over my hair and sighed heavily. My pops was right. It didn't matter how many plans I made for myself, God was always going to guide my steps. I could fight it for as long as I wanted to, but eventually I was going to have to surrender.

"I'm not going to sit here and act like I want to do this, Pastor Stanford."

He chuckled and placed his hands in his pockets.

"No one ever truly does. No one who knows the weight of it all. If

92

He didn't plan on equipping you He wouldn't have called you, Hunter. How are things going with Onyx?"

A smile immediately covered my face. That was my baby. I couldn't wait to make her my wife. And be able to go to sleep next to her and wake up next to her. And be able to work on my films as she painted or drew. And be able to kiss her and make love to her whenever I wanted to. And be able to plant a few seeds in her womb.

That reminded me; we need to talk about how many babies she plans on giving me.

"Things are going great with us. She was giving me a hard time at first, and trying her hardest to deny how she felt, but she's letting me in now."

"Good. That's good. Really good."

The sadness that filled his eyes was hard to ignore. I couldn't imagine how it felt to not speak to your granddaughter for years. It was no secret that it was hard on her, but I never thought about how difficult it may have been for him.

"Have you tried reaching out to her?"

"No use. Since I… she won't speak to me."

I never understood how he could have turned his back on her. I mean… I get that her lifestyle probably wasn't the one he wanted for her, but still. I don't care how close I get to God; I just can't see myself turning my back on my family.

Not if their actions weren't hindering my relationship with God.

"She misses you."

"Did she say that?"

"I can tell. She didn't say it exactly, but she does."

I didn't want to tell him that she spent practically every night at the church. Figured that was something she'd tell him herself if she wanted him to know.

"Well, I don't regret much, but turning my back on her is the one thing I don't think I'll ever forgive myself for."

"Come on, Pastor Stanford, you know that's no way to live."

"I know. I know that in my mind, but in my heart..." Pastor Stanford scratched his neck and stood. "I don't want to hold you up. I just wanted to come by and talk to you for a second."

I stood and walked him to the door. My plan was to leave early enough to stop and get Onyx one of those cake pop things from Starbucks, but I wasn't sure if I'd have time now. No, I was going to make time.

-&-

Onyx surprised was the most adorable thing I'd ever seen. When I stopped by her place she was still sleep. Rubbing her eyes as she opened the door. She looked at me and smiled before grabbing the cake pop out of my hand and jumping into my arms. Between her bites she planted kisses all over my face. I ended up having to carry her to my car as she ate so I could leave.

The sight of her smile kept reappearing in my head throughout the day; and each time it did I couldn't help but smile. Was this love?

"What's got you all smiley?" Michelle asked from behind me.

I still hadn't checked her for calling my folks when I was arrested.

With Michelle, she just would have found a way to justify what she did. Ignoring her worked best.

"Thinking about my girl," I answered honestly as I prepared to take my lunchbreak.

"Your girl?"

Michelle took a step back, and her face was laced with confusion.

"Yea. My girl."

"I didn't know you were in a relationship. You told me you weren't trying to be in a relationship."

"I told you that I wasn't trying to be in a relationship with a woman that I didn't see myself marrying."

"So… you're gonna marry her?"

I finally stopped fiddling with my papers and gave her my full attention.

"Michelle…"

"Don't bullshit me, Hunter. Just be straight up with me. I don't need you to spare my feelings."

"Fine. If it's within my power, I'm going to marry Onyx."

"Onyx? Stanford? The stripper?"

"She's not a stripper."

"But that's her?"

I nodded and ran my hand down the back of my neck.

"Wow. Okay." She chuckled softly and took a step back. "What does she have that I don't?"

I shrugged and took a step back.

"My heart. My mind. My attention. Me being with her goes beyond us. Our relationship is one of love, yes, but more than anything purpose. No one is going to stand in the way of that. Not even ourselves and our past. I'm sorry if my mother fed you false hope of there ever being something between us, but I've made it clear since I started working here that I wanted us to be nothing but coworkers, Michelle."

"But you won't even give us a chance. You act like I'm not worth you, but I know I am."

"Your worth has nothing to do with it. Don't ever base your worth on whether you have a man or not. I'm not for you. That's not a reflection of you or your worth. We're just not meant to be together. There is a man out there that's going to adore you just as much as I adore my baby. That doesn't take away from you at all, sweetie. That just means I'm not the one."

"But you're so fine, and so good, and so sweet…" Michelle chuckled and shook her head. "But you're right. I'm tripping. I just… like you so much. And I thought if I was patient enough that one day I'd get my chance with you. I guess not, huh?"

"No. I'm sorry."

She nodded and looked at me for a couple of seconds before walking away. I felt so bad, but it was better to just let her know that she had absolutely no chance than to lead her on like my mother had been doing for years. Michelle was an attractive woman. There was no doubt in my mind that she would soon find the perfect man for her. It just wasn't gon be me.

Onyx

"Tell me your secrets and I'll tell you mine. Every truth, every lie. Every wrong, every right. Every heartbreak, every setback. Every mistake, every crime."

My baby called me on his break and told me about the day he'd been having, so I wanted to do something special for him to take his mind off of things when he got home. I'd spent my day job hunting, and I had a couple of solid leads along with three interviews for later in the week. Two were in Memphis, and the other was in New York.

I don't know what the hell made me apply for the job in New York. I guess because it was my way of convincing myself that I didn't feel as strongly as I do for Hunter. But that shit didn't work. Just the thought of leaving him was torturous, so I knew that was something I'd never really be able to do.

"Make me your confidant. Make me best friend. If you lose or if you win. If you're a saint or if you sin. And if I don't understand I'll do the best that I can."

I had Chrisette Michele going in the background. The lights were down low. My candles were going. And the steak and potatoes I fixed had the house smelling good as hell. My doorbell rang, and even though I was expecting Hunter I still jumped. It didn't matter how much time I spent with him I still couldn't believe he wanted me.

"Some people search high and low, for someone who makes them whole. So I'm not letting go."

When I opened the door and saw him I couldn't help but smile. He stepped inside and pecked my lips tenderly before grabbing my ass and biting down on his lip.

"Hunter Hendrix," I spoke.

He smiled and released me so I could close the door.

"Hey, baby. You got it smelling good in here. What you cook?"

"Steak, potatoes and onions, and corn on the cob. It's a salad in there too."

"That sounds good. I'm starving. How was your day?"

I leaned against the table and watched as he opened the bottle of wine I had on the counter.

"Cause you mean that much to me. So take all this love from me. I'm giving you every part of me. All of this heart in me. Here is my offering"

"It was cool. Got a call for another interview."

"That's great, Onyx. I'm really happy for you."

I twisted my mouth to the side and considered telling him that it was in New York, but I held it back.

"How was your day? Did it get any better after your encounter with Michelle?"

He sighed heavily as he poured us both a glass of wine.

"Yea. I talked to you."

See, this is what had me falling in love with him. The simplicity yet magnitude of his feelings for me. He wasn't just talking or trying to run game. You could see it in his eyes that he meant that shit. And I couldn't help but blush as I walked over to him. The second I was within arms reached, Hunter wrapped his arm around me and pulled me into him.

He kissed my temple and I returned it with a kiss to his neck.

"I talked to your grandfather today too." I tried to remove myself from his grip, but he held me tighter. "No running."

"I'll be your refuge. Be your sanctuary. Be your peace like a dove. Like a prayer. Like a hug. And if that don't do the trick I came equipped with my love."

With a deep breath, I crossed my arms over my chest. His petty ass pushed them down.

"Hunter, I really don't care about you talking to him. I don't want to talk about you talking to him."

"Why not?"

"Because I don't."

"Even if it was about you?"

I was interested… but not enough to take it there with him. The scar that my grandfather left with his rejection was the biggest of all. I guess because… he was the one I clung to most. In his attempt to help my parents straighten me out he strained our relationship. And just when I thought it couldn't get any worse he told me it was my lifestyle or him.

Then, he didn't even give me the chance to choose. He made the choice for me. Told me to never step foot in his house or his church again. I guess in his effort to keep me from rejecting me, he rejected me.

"Ask of me anything. Any gift any kind. Any reason any time. Any need or any size. And if you need more I'll search 'til I find."

"He misses you, Onyx. He has pictures of you in his office and home that he just stares at. He still hasn't forgiven himself for turning his back on you. I think if you talked to him… he'd beg for your forgiveness and give you the closure you need."

"Hunter…"

"If not for him or for you, do it for me. Please."

I massaged my temples as my head began to throb. I can't lie… life without the baggage of my past would be nice… but could it really have been as simple talking to him and forgiving him?

"Please, Onyx."

Hunter took my face into his hands and started covering it with kisses, and even if I wanted to say no I couldn't at this point.

"Fine. Fine. I'll talk to him. For two minutes. And you have to be there."

"You know I'll be there with you, Onyx."

"Okay. I guess I'll call him and… see what I can set up."

"Good. I know you won't regret it. Now, fix me a plate so we can eat and then go to the bowling alley. Get your losses out the way."

"Mane, whatever. Ima beat you in bowling just like I beat you in poker last night."

"Girl, please. You won one game; and you only won that one because I let you."

Hunter

"There's something I need to tell you," Onyx mumbled as she ran her hand down the invisible wrinkles she thought were on her dress for the millionth time.

A week had passed since she agreed to speak to her grandfather, and the day had finally come.

"What's up?" I asked.

I opened the door of the church and let her step in first. Once inside, she turned to face me. Her fingers intertwined in the center of her as her head lowered.

"Umm…" Her eyes met mine briefly before she looked to the left and inhaled deeply. "You know my interview next Monday?"

"Yea… what about it?"

Her eyes met mine again, and they were filled with uncertainty. I took her hand into mine and caressed it with my thumb.

"What's up, baby? Spit it out."

She took another deep breath before taking my free hand into hers.

"Umm… it's… in New York."

I couldn't even reply right away. For a second I just looked at her. She was bout to make me lose my religion. What was she taking an interview in a completely different state for???

"Say something…" she pleaded softly.

"Onyx?"

I looked up, and she turned around to face Pastor Stanford. It looked as if her breath had come out of her. She inhaled deeply and her body swayed like she was about to pass out. Even though her confession had messed up my mental, I wrapped my arm around her waist to steady her.

Pastor Stanford took a step forward, and she took a step back.

"Baby girl…"

Pastor Stanford took another step forward, and she took another step back. She grabbed my hand and squeezed it. I said a quick, silent prayer for her strength, then kissed the side of her forehead. Onyx looked up at me and her watery eyes made my heart skip a beat.

"It's okay," I assured her with a gentle squeeze of her hand.

"I'm glad you came," Pastor Stanford said.

She didn't answer him. She just… stepped behind me a little.

"I'm so sorry, baby girl. I should have never turned my back against you. I was just… hurting. My baby girl was living a reckless life and… I didn't know how to handle it. I couldn't stomach it. I didn't know how to handle you growing up and making those bad decisions. I didn't handle you and the situation in a loving and peaceful way.

I allowed my fear of what my church would say and the embarrassment to cause me to turn you away. For that, I apologize. Will you ever be able to forgive me? There's… there's nothing more important to me right now than rebuilding my relationship with you. If you give me a chance… I will never break your heart and trust again."

I looked at her and tears were streaming down her face.

"You. You. You. That's all I heard was you. How what I was doing affected you. Did you ever think about me for me? Why I was doing what I was doing? I treasured you, Grandpa. And you made me feel like shi – like I was nothing," she confessed through her sob. "Do you know what it feels like to be rejected by those you love and want to please most?" He shook his head and lowered it. "And what? You get to say you're sorry and that's supposed to just make everything okay?"

"I'm not saying me saying I'm sorry will make this better, Onyx, but I was praying that it would be a start. I was praying that… you'd grace me with your presence again and I'd be able to show you how sorry I was. How much I love you and miss you and value you, baby girl. I'm just asking for your time and a chance to show you how committed I am to making this right."

Onyx looked at me… like she needed my approval. I nodded and pushed her forward slightly. She released my hand and took another step towards Pastor Stanford.

"I'm sorry, baby girl. I love you. I'm so sorry. Please, forgive me."

"Okay," she whispered softly with a nod. "I… I forgive you."

His shoulders slumped. As if the weight of the world had been removed from them. Pastor Stanford stepped forward and pulled Onyx into his arms. They held each other tightly and cried. Each telling the other how sorry they were. And as much as I didn't want to… I shed a couple of tears too.

Onyx

*I*t seemed like... after I talked things over with my grandpa... I was on this loving forgiving spree. I worked things out with my grandma, and talked things through with my parents. I let them know finally that I was done with stripping and looking into a career that would allow me to use my degree.

Since I told Hunter about my interview in New York he'd been kind of distant. He still called and we still kicked it... but there was something that was off. He wasn't his normal open self. I wasn't expecting him to take the interview to heart. I mean... it was just an interview. It wasn't anything set in stone.

I hadn't been offered the job. And even if I was offered the job who's to say I would actually take it?

Every time I tried to talk to him about it he brushed me off. Which was weird because he'd always been open and honest with me. Even about things I didn't want to hear or talk about. I talked him into taking me to the airport, even though it was clear he didn't want to, and he avoided my eyes the entire drive there and as he carried my bags inside.

Once I had my checked bag checked in I walked over to him and found him absently staring into his phone.

"Hey," I spoke softly to gain his attention.

He looked up at me with empty eyes before smiling with half of his mouth and returning his attention to his phone.

"You good to go?"

I nodded, and he didn't see me, but that didn't stop him from pecking on that damn phone long enough to look at me. I started to grab that shit and toss it across the room since he had a little funky attitude. But I couldn't even be mad at him because he was feeling some type of way over the decision I made.

"Can I have a hug and kiss goodbye so you can go since you're more interested in your phone than me?"

Hunter looked at me with his head tilted to the side for a few seconds before shaking his head and chuckling. He put his phone into his pocket and lifted my face with his pointing finger under my chin. The kiss that he placed on my lips was quick and unlike him before he pulled me into his chest and gave me the softest hug he'd ever given me.

"Be safe, Onyx. Let me know when you land. Call me once you've checked into your room."

"What's your problem, Hunter?"

"What's my problem?"

"Yea. What's your problem?"

"Nothing. I guess I'll see you when you get back. If you're coming back. Are you coming back?"

"Of course I'm coming back. Why wouldn't I?"

"If you get the job... what's left to keep you here?"

I sighed and he put some space between us. Which was weird in itself because he was always getting closer to me... not pulling himself away.

"I have you." He chuckled and shook his head as his eyes went to the side of me. "My stuff is here. My family is here. I am trying to rebuild with them." I sighed and ran my hand over my stomach. "I don't even know why I'm going for this interview," I mumbled more to myself than to him.

That got his attention.

"You're going because this is something you want, right? This is a great opportunity. Twenty thousand more than what you'd be making if you took either of the jobs that you were offered here. And... it's New York. Why wouldn't you go?"

"I don't have any experience..."

"But your portfolio is amazing. You're amazing, Onyx."

"But I don't have any experience. The only work experience I have is stripping and I couldn't put that on my resume. And I'm pretty sure getting money out of old dudes doesn't make me look qualified to be an art buyer. I'm setting myself up for failure. I don't even know why they called me for an interview."

Hunter closed the space between us and lifted my head. I hadn't even realized I'd lowered it.

"You never see yourself as greatly as those around you do, Onyx. I'm sure that's why you got the call. Because God is trying to show you just how amazing you are. I guess maybe I couldn't, so maybe this job will."

"Hunter, you do…"

He silenced me with a kiss and rested his forehead on mine.

"I want you to go to that interview with confidence. Not in yourself, but in God. In the God in you. You can do all things through Christ who is your strength. You were fearfully and wonderfully made, baby. You're a masterpiece. You have the creativity of the Creator inside of you. You have an eye for art, and you create masterpieces. *That's what they saw in you and your portfolio.*

Don't go out there with a defeated spirit because you'll be giving that energy off to the universe and you'll screw yourself up. I want you to go in there like the job is already yours. Because it is. And when something or someone is yours… there is nothing that can be done to stop you from having it."

I nodded as he wiped tears from my cheeks. How was I going to leave this man? Why did I put myself in the position to have to leave this man? Here he was encouraging me and being all sweet when it was clear that me leaving was tearing him up inside. But he put me first. And I needed to do the same.

"Thank you, Hunter. For everything. I'm not doing this because I'm not happy here. Because I'm not happy here with you. I don't know why I'm doing this."

I scratched the back of my ear and stopped talking to avoid crying again. He didn't say anything. Just looked at me. Like he was trying to memorize my face.

"You're detaching yourself from me. Why?"

He shrugged and placed his hands in his pockets.

"Just… think it'll be better this way; you know? If you leave… I'll have to get used to not having you anyway. I'll see you when you get back, okay?"

I nodded and wrapped my arms around him. Buried my head in his chest. He let me stay there for a moment before wrapping his hands around my neck and tilting my head up. He placed a soft kiss on my forehead, then released me. I watched him walk away and was filled with a feeling of guilt. What had I done?

Hunter

The last four days had honestly been a blur. I tried desperately to not overthink the whole New York situation and not take it personally, but I can't lie… it kind of felt like a slap in the face.

Like… I'd been spending all of this time trying to get her to see that I was committed to her, but it felt as if she wasn't as committed to me. As into me as I was into her. Yea, I knew in my mind that she needed this opportunity. She needed this fresh start. But in my heart… my heart just wanted her. Here. With me. But I would never say that to her; nor would I try and keep her from moving.

If anyone deserved a fresh start it was Onyx; and I refused to stand in the way of that.

As I sat in my car and waited for her outside of the airport I couldn't help but think about how differently my life was going to be after she left. In just a short period of time, she'd come into my life and shook it up in a way that I would have never expected. I'd gotten so used to having her… I just… couldn't see my life without her in it from this point forward.

But there was no doubt in my mind that she'd gotten the job.

When I saw her, I got out of the car and met her to grab her bags. Well, to hug and kiss and hold her for a second – then grab her bags.

The first few seconds of the ride were silent. When I couldn't take it anymore I looked over at her and asked…

"So… how did it go?"

She looked at me and smiled.

"They… loved my portfolio. And how familiar with the company and industry I was. My second day there, they sent me to an auction. They were impressed with the piece I'd chosen. I was able to convince the potential buyer to pay twice the price we purchased it for my third day there."

"So… you got the job?"

Onyx nodded and smiled again.

"Yes. I… I got the job."

"That's great, Onyx. You deserve it, baby. I'm so happy for you."

Her smile fell and she looked out of her window.

"You're not mad?"

"Of course not. I'm going to miss you like crazy, but you deserve this fresh start."

"I could stay here. The position to appraise art and restore antiques really is a good position. And I was promised a ten thousand dollar raise every year until I reached my cap. So, I would end up making what I could be making in New York here," she said… as if she was reasoning within herself more than she was talking to me.

I felt like she wanted me to okay her staying here… but I wasn't going to do that. I couldn't do that. I didn't want her staying here just to be with me and then she ends up resenting me.

"Hunter…"

"I'm not comfortable agreeing with that, Onyx. New York is a great opportunity."

"But…" She looked at me briefly before looking back out of the window. "But I don't want to leave you. Why did I put us in this position?"

I grabbed her hand and she looked at me with saddened eyes.

"I've learned that things aren't always what they seem. Maybe this was never meant to be forever for us. Maybe I was brought into your life to just… help you get on a different path in life. I mean, look at how different and positive things are for you now. If that was the purpose of me coming into your life I'm more than happy with that."

"So, you're not even going to fight for us?"

"Fight for us?" I repeated louder than I wanted to.

I was trying my hardest to keep my cool. To not make her feel bad about bettering herself. To not express the fact that I felt like she just tossed what we were building to the side.

"Why should I fight for us when you're the one that put what we had on the line? What do you want me to do, Onyx? Beg you to stay?"

"I want you to act like you care, Hunter. Not like you don't care either way."

"Baby… it's not that I don't care. I'm just… not going to hold you back. Of course I care. Of course I want you. I want what's best for you. If that's this job in New York I'm more than willing to stand down and let you have that."

She shook her head in disbelief and returned her attention outside of the window. I cut the radio up and the rest of the drive was done in silence. Fight for us. Fight for us? Why should I have to fight for us? This was her doing. Her decision. If anyone needed to be doing the fighting it was her.

What? Since I was the man and the leader it's my responsibility to put my heart on the line and beg her to stay when there's obviously something in her that wants to go? Nah. I'm straight on that.

I pulled up in front of her apartment and asked, "When are they expecting you back?"

"Two weeks," she mumbled as she unbuckled her seatbelt.

"Two weeks?"

My heart started racing and my surprise was evident in the distressed tone of my voice. Two weeks? All we had left was two weeks? I quickly popped my trunk and got out of the car to get some fresh air because I swear it felt like I was suffocating inside of there with her.

I carried her bags to her front door, and she didn't get out of the car until I leaned against the door. Slowly, she made her way to me. Her head lifted and she looked into my eyes until I moved to the side so she could unlock the door. Once she had it open I took her bags inside and tried to make my way back out but she grabbed my hand.

"Are you leaving already? I just got back home. I want to spend some time with you."

"I started a short film while you were gone that I need to edit. Besides, I think we should stop spending as much time together. Since you're leaving soon."

Her eyebrows wrinkled as she wrapped her hands around my wrists.

"I really need you to stay, Hunter Hendrix, please. I know I'm being selfish right now… but I really don't want you to go. I missed you. A lot. Please stay. Or I'll come to your place. You can get your edits done and I'll just… be there. We don't even have to be in the same room. I just… need to be near you."

Everything in me told me to say no. That I would be setting myself up to be even more hurt when she left. But there was nothing I wouldn't do for this girl. So as much as I wanted to say no and prepare myself to be without her I said yes.

She grabbed her smaller bag in one hand and took my hand in the other before leading me back out of her apartment and to my car.

Onyx

$\mathcal{T}$wo weeks had never gone by so quickly in my life. There was a constant tug of war going on between Hunter and I. He was trying to push me away while I was trying to pull him closer. I felt bad as hell for putting him in this position. He was trying his hardest to get me out of his system; but I wasn't having that shit.

If he thought he was going to be able to just let me go and forget he ever knew me he had another thing coming. We hadn't really discussed what was going to become of us once I left. To be honest, I'd been avoiding that conversation. He tried to talk about it a couple of times, but I quickly shut that down.

Hunter was standing outside waiting for me to get out at the airport, but I really didn't want to. I looked down at the multicolor slides I had on and thought about when we went to Waffle House the second night we talked. The thought of him picking me up and carrying me out of the restaurant made me smile. I looked up at him and tears immediately filled my eyes.

"Onyx…"

"I can't do this, Hunter. I can't leave you."

"Baby, please go."

"You don't want me anymore?"

Hunter kneeled in front of me as my tears began to fall.

"Of course I want you. I will always want you. I love you." His head lowered as he grabbed my hands. I lifted it and he continued to speak. "But I don't want to hold you back. I don't want you resenting me. I want you to do what's best for you. This is an amazing opportunity, Onyx. I wouldn't feel right if you didn't take it."

"You love me?"

Nothing that he said after that registered in my brain to be honest. He smiled and caressed my cheek with his thumb.

"I love you," he repeated.

"See... that's... that's good. Because... last night I couldn't sleep. And... I was thinking. You know... what if... what if I went through all of this because I felt like I didn't deserve you because I wasn't good enough for you?"

"Onyx..."

"All I've ever been is the Preacher's troubled prostitute granddaughter. So for a man like you to want me and see me so beautifully... that scared me, Hunter. I didn't want to wake up one day and you see me the way everyone else does.

I didn't want to wake up one day and you realize you deserve better than me. I just... wanted to do something and be someone that you would be proud of."

"But I am proud of you. You think I care about what you used to do to make your money? That's not who you are. That doesn't define you."

"I know. I know that now. But when I was filling out those applications… I just wanted to be… good for you. And when the New York office called me it made me feel so damn good, but I overlooked the fact that I would have to leave you and work there."

His eyes watered, and I took his face into the palms of my hands.

"I just wanted to be better for you, Hunter. But this job means nothing to me if I can't have you. And I know when I leave… things are eventually going to fizzle out between us, and I don't want to let you go. I can work here with no problem, but if I can't have you there… I don't want to be there. And I love you too."

"You went through all of this for me?"

I nodded as he pulled me out of the car.

"I don't want to say I'm proud of you. I don't want to say I love you. I don't want to say I want to be with you." Each word felt like a bulldozer hitting my chest. Pummeling my heart. "I want to show you."

"What?"

Hunter kneeled before me and I damn near peed myself.

"I don't have a ring, yet, but I'll get one. Today. And I'll give you a special proposal. But I don't want another day to pass by without you being my wife. I love you, Onyx Stanford. Just the way you are. And I want to spend the rest of my life showing you that. So…"

"Yes!"

I yelled and jumped and hugged him tightly all at the same time. Hunter laughed and tried to remove my arms from around his neck but I was holding on for dear life.

"Baby… let me ask you. You're worth this. Let me get it out."

Unwillingly, I released the hold I had on him and stood upright. He inhaled deeply as he took my hands into his.

"Onyx… will you marry me?"

Now I was speechless. I nodded adamantly as tears poured from my eyes. Hunter stood, pulled me into his arms, and kissed me deeper than he ever had before.

EPILOGUE

Onyx

$\mathcal{H}$unter Hendrix was my husband. My backbone. My inspiration to do and be good. Our wedding was in the church, and that was the first time I'd been in there during the day in years. My grandfather officiated. And surprisingly, Hunter's parents attended.

His father was all smiles as he welcomed me into his family. With open arms, he vowed to be as close as a second father to me. Shantel wasn't as open, but she was pleasant and respectful so that was a great start.

My grandfather wasted no time telling Hunter that as soon as we came back from our honeymoon he wanted to start mentoring him and preparing him to take his spot as Pastor. He wanted Hunter to be ordained within the next year. But with his ordination came me being a First Lady. Me? Nah. Ion know about that.

God was definitely going to have to complete the work he'd started in me for that.

But for now, I was taking this thing one day at a time. Praying and trying to talk to Him more throughout my day. Starting and ending it reading my bible with Hunter. It wasn't much… but it was progress… and the peace that I felt let me know that God was pleased with that.

I'd never been nervous about having sex with a man. Not even when I gave away my virginity. But as I watched Hunter undress… I was scared. Maybe because I felt like what we were about to experience was going to go beyond sex.

I'd been waiting for this since I met him… and now that it was here… now that he was mine and I was his… my ass was scared of the dick!

He must have sensed it because he smiled as he pushed his boxers down.

"We can take this as slow as we need to," he assured me.

My eyes lowered to the gift between his thighs and I had to silently thank God for blessing me with a man that was literally the perfect package for me. I knew that there was no such thing as a perfect person or a perfect love… but Hunter Hendrix was perfect for *me*.

And his dick looked like it would fit perfectly *into* me. I watched as he slowly made his way to the bed, and I couldn't take my eyes off of his dick.

I mean… I knew that it was nice sized from feeling it through his shorts a couple of times… but it was beautiful. The perfect shade. The perfect length. The perfect width. The perfect curve. It was perfect.

Hunter made his way on top of me, and the feel of his dick against my clit had me moaning and biting down on my lip. I was wet as hell already, and it was only going to get worse. His lips covered mine, and before I knew it, he hands were all over me. Gripping my neck. My thighs. My breasts. Against my clit.

His tongue was out of my mouth and following the same trail his hands had taken.

Each caress of his hands and his tongue had my back arching and my nerves unraveling.

And then... he made his way between my legs... and the smile that covered his face let me know that this church boy was about to turn my ass out!

THE END!

A NOTE FROM B...

Hey y'all!

So... if you didn't notice... this book is kind of based on Hosea and Gomer in the bible. This is what I would call a modern day bible story with a B. Love twist! For those of you that have followed my writing career... you should be familiar with my story Love Me Until I Love Myself: Sage and Delilah's Love Story.

That was my first modern day bible story. Now, it is just a straight up urban Christian romance. It was so well received, and I vowed to do more... but... I wanted to do something different. Something more authentic. Something more me.

And that's exactly what I did when writing Hunter and Onyx's story! It's urban, and Onyx is definitely a character... but Hunter... Hunter is everything! If I could write stories like this for the rest of my writing career, I would! I hope you were able to catch on to the overall theme of this book – the acceptance that comes from true unconditional love.

Well, I'd love to hear what you thought about the book! Connect with me via social media and let me know! Thank you so much for reading! Muah!

Love,

B. Love

Join my Facebook group for discussions, giveaways, sneak peeks, and more!

https://www.facebook.com/groups/1692462904324931/

Author Page - www.facebook.com/authorblove

Instagram – www.instagram.com/authorblove

Twitter – www.twitter.com/authorblove

Looking for a publishing home?

Royalty Publishing House, Where the Royals reside, is accepting submissions for writers in the urban fiction genre. If you're interested, submit the first 3-4 chapters with your synopsis to submissions@royaltypublishinghouse.com.

Check out our website for more information: www.royaltypublishinghouse.com.

Text ROYALTY to 42828 to join our mailing list!

To submit a manuscript for our review, email us at
submissions@royaltypublishinghouse.com

Text RPHCHRISTIAN to 22828 for our
CHRISTIAN ROMANCE novels!

Text RPHROMANCE to 22828 for our
INTERRACIAL ROMANCE novels!

Get LiT!

Download the LiT app today and enjoy exclusive content, free books, and more

Do You Like CELEBRITY GOSSIP?

Check Out QUEEN DYNASTY!
Visit Our Site: www.thequeendynasty.com

CPSIA information can be obtained
at www.ICGtesting.com
Printed in the USA
LVOW10s2024050217

523261LV00016B/929/P

9 781542 454889